THIEF

Published by Salty Dog Press
Edited by Paulene Turner
Cover design by Holly Dunn
Copyright © Salty Dog Press, 2026

Salty Dog Press acknowledges the traditional owners of the country in which we live and work. We pay our respects to all Aboriginal and Torres Strait Islander Elders, past and present.

THIEF

Edited by

Paulene Turner

Salty Dog Press

*Dedicated to writers everywhere...
fighting to keep imagination alive
one story at a time*

Editor's foreword

I've always been fascinated by thieves. Not so much the grubby real-life ones who break into your home or pinch your wallet when you're not looking. But stories of stylish criminals with grand aspirations. Stealing priceless necklaces from well-guarded vaults. Escaping across rooftops with the police clambering after them. The robbers who work as a team distracting here, while their comrades purloin there, in a plan so clever it would leave Sherlock Holmes scratching his head.

Think *Ocean's Eleven*, *The Thomas Crown Affair*, *The Italian Job*. The thief is a romantic figure in fiction. Many commit wrong acts for the right reasons—bringing heartless corporations to justice or using wealth gained illicitly for benevolent purposes. Or perhaps they just couldn't resist something shiny?

They're chancers with a twinkle in their eye and a diamond necklace in their top pocket. Who can resist?

Such stories promise danger and excitement. And isn't that why we read books? To have an up-close view of someone attempting to do things that we dare not? Pulling off an impossible steal requires tremendous bravery and specialist skill. Though the thieves are a tad bad and breaking the rules, we can't help but admire their courage in reaching for the stars, regardless of the consequences.

The thieves in this volume come in all shapes and styles.

From a grand heist across the galaxy in Jessica Wilcox's epic *A Con for the Legends* and a daring theft by two tightrope walkers in

Miguel A. Rueda's *Highwire Heist*, to a meeting of devious minds on a train in the Old West in *Three Tickets to Telluride* by Nikki Blakely.

There are poignant moments where the thief must face the consequences of their actions in *Almost Forget* by MM Schreier and *Daily Dozen* by Myna Chang. And a tense stand-off between a group of thieves dividing up the spoils after a big job in Trey Dowell's *Honor, Thieves, Etc.* Lisa Fox reveals the harsh, unglamorous reality of a life spent trying to blend in but never belonging in *Camouflage*. While, in *My Legacy*, Andrea Goyan gives us a view behind the scenes at the rhythms of an illicit life.

If you love a hard-boiled private eye—as I do—you'll relish *The Cherry-Pie Files* by Trond E. Hildahl. A touch of fantasy? Try Heather Santo's enchanting *The Scarf Thief* or Patsy Pratt-Herzog's *Good Manners* (you'll smile when you reach the point in the story where you 'get' the title). And Alex Turner-Cohen presents a dazzling dystopian world in *The Happiness Thief*.

There's humor too. You'll laugh out loud in *A Safe Place* by Faye Upton (who has two stories in the collection!), filled with super-smart future tech, and *When Men Wear Pink* by Leslie Muzingo, with not-so-smart (but definitely fun) schemers.

Some historical fiction steals in, too, with S.L. Kretschmer's moving *The Final Portrait* and my own story, *The Mysterious Smile*, about a trip through time to visit Leonardo da Vinci.

And of course there's romance—in *Let's Taco 'Bout Love*, Nora Fry's cute tale of rival food trucks, and *Steal My Heart* from the POV of a detective in pursuit of a master criminal by Bea Sage.

The memorable *Odessa* by the prolific and talented R.A. Clarke finishes off the collection. (Bring your tissues!)

The stories vary in length, motivation, and writing style but they're all worth reading. Together, they cover the theme of 'thief' in a myriad of ways.

Take a look at the writers' biographies and you'll see they're all highly experienced with numerous awards between them. Many have had short stories in some of the world's leading publications. Others have penned novels, short plays, and screenplays.

These are the types of people who are always writing one thing, imagining another—words swimming in their heads from a tide of ideas, a tsunami of inspiration. They look through the window and see, not their neighbor's bulging trash cans, but knights in a medieval tournament, pirates clutching the rigging in a storm at sea, a sun setting behind an alien skyline. They eschew the beach on sunny days to sit in dark offices staring at screens in search of a brilliant plot twist, a more affecting description, a deeper meaning. They've put in the work and are now highly skilled in their chosen art.

I'm proud to gather this wonderful work in one exciting collection and hope you enjoy reading these rich tales as much as I have done.

Paulene Turner
Salty Dog Press

CONTENTS

A Con for the Legends

BY JESSICA WILCOX

The Vesperin Drift was quieter than Bragg expected, the kind of hush that swallowed noise and left only the faint thrum of *The Rook*'s engines for company. Outside the viewscreen, the debris field stretched on for kilometers—a slow-moving graveyard of shattered hulls, cracked cargo crates, and the skeletal frames of long-dead transports. Scraps of reflective metal spun lazily in the thin light of the distant star, catching glints like broken glass. A half-collapsed mining barge drifted by at an angle, its interior gutted and exposed, cables wavering like deep-sea tentacles. Everything moved with a strange, eerie grace, as if the wreckage were performing a slow, perpetual dance around *The Rook*.

And beyond that swirling halo of ruin—past the drifting panels, the frozen droplets of coolant, and a stray cargo net turning in the void—a glimmer of steady light, too smooth to be junk and too deliberate to be chance, hovered at the far edge of the screen. Nestled beyond the debris cloud like an eye peeking through curtains of wreckage was a small pod, matte and unmarked except for the faint blue pulse at its hinge. Ferro's pod. The only thing in the Drift that still had a heartbeat.

"There it is." Captain Talia Bragg leaned forward in her chair, boots planted wide on the grated deck as *The Rook* drifted through the debris-choked fringe, humming in quiet defiance. Static shimmered along the forward shields, catching flecks of frozen metal and abandoned cargo like fireflies.

A squat, ugly little vessel—more engine than elegance—with armor plating that looked hammered on by someone in a hurry and a cockpit that jutted forward like a broken tooth. *The Rook*'s hull was a patchwork of scorched metal and salvaged panels in three different shades of gunmetal, the starboard thruster still bearing the dent from their last run-in with Customs. But she was fast, stubborn, and loud enough to make bigger cruisers think twice.

"I told you she was out here, Betty," Bragg murmured, reaching to the screen as if she could touch the pod. It was the lead she'd been chasing for weeks—and the reason she'd dragged *The Rook* into the most notorious graveyard in the sector.

"We all knew Ferro was out here." B377Y rolled her eyes as she lounged in the copilot's seat like she owned it, her tall, silver frame all elbows and mismatched joints, one long leg kicked out as if daring the console to object. A strip of faded hazard tape was wrapped around one arm, and half her cranial plating didn't match the rest.

"But the chances of finding her were 678,432 to one." V3R0N1C4 hovered behind them with the stiff poise of a retired casino hostess, her squat gold-and-black chassis clicking softly as her processors whirred. She was a walking patchwork of spare parts and questionable upgrades, but her voice was smooth as velvet.

"I told you that I defy all odds." Bragg rose, stepping closer to the viewscreen. "And keep my promises."

"Six months too late." B377Y couldn't feel like a human did, but her capacity for sarcasm was off the chart.

"Less cheek, Betty, more thrust."

As B377Y navigated them closer, the dot resolved into a small, pill-shaped object. Captain Bragg traced it across the screen with her thick fingers. The life-support pod grew on the screen as they got closer and she imagined she could see Ferro through the thick window, sleeping peacefully.

When the ship got close enough, she turned back to B377Y.

"Prepare the tractor beam to pull her in."

"Yes, Captain." The android turned around, metal lip curling up to reveal the dark cavern of her voice tube. "You better go wash up before waking her. No one is falling into your arms looking like that."

"And you shouldn't make that face anymore," Bragg glowered back. "That face would give nightmares to small children."

Bragg scratched the palms of her hands as she walked toward her quarters. She shouldn't be this nervous. She was rescuing Ferro, after all—bringing her back, same as she'd promised before the whole con went sideways.

She could have left Ferro drifting through the periphery forever, but that wasn't her style. Bragg didn't fail. Not at love, not at cons, and definitely not at grand heists involving the Emperor himself.

◆

Bragg had spent most of her teens doing drudge work on bigger ships in the Central Galaxy, but she always dreamed of captaining her own. Her small, stout figure not only made her perfect for crawling in and out of small spaces, of which there were many on spaceships, but it also kept her from receiving unwanted attention from certain male crew members.

That was how she met Ferro.

Heading back to her bunk, tired after a long shift, Bragg barely noticed a man and woman arguing in the passage until the woman grabbed her arm and pulled her into a tight embrace followed by a long kiss on the mouth.

"Oh, there you are, Talia!" She kept Bragg's arm tightly clasped in her own. "I was just explaining to this... nice lieutenant that you'd be along any minute and here you are!"

Bragg looked wide-eyed at the woman. Her mouth opened and closed like a fish, but no sound came out.

Ferro was stunning in the way stars were—bright, distant, and dangerous to look at for too long. Tall and long-limbed, with skin the deep, warm brown of sun-baked stone and eyes that shimmered like molten copper when she was amused. Her features were elegant and sharp, softened only by the faint iridescent sheen beneath her skin that hinted at something inhuman. Even exhausted from her shift, she looked like someone carved for the sole purpose of being impossible to ignore.

"It's okay, honey, you look exhausted, we'll just go." She swept her shiny, long, dark hair off her shoulder, revealing her identification badge—Ferro Klow, Hostess.

Bragg looked down at her own badge feeling dense, realizing that's how this woman, Ferro, knew her name. She looked back and forth between Ferro and the lieutenant. "What's happening here?"

"Hold on a minute," the lieutenant butted in. "I've never seen you two together. In fact, I've never seen you with a woman, Ferro, but you've dated half the men on board."

"Not just men, Gerrick." Ferro pointed a finger in his face. "I don't think Drax would appreciate it if he heard you calling him a man."

Lieutenant Gerrick's face went a little green and he stepped back, hands in the air. "No, you're probably right."

She shook, and scales rippled out across her body before flipping back to her rich, dark skin.

Bragg blinked, still trying to make sense of what was happening. She'd grown up around Nexarians, but it still startled her when they shifted. She opened her mouth to talk again, but Ferro was already pulling her away.

"Come on, sugar, let's get you to bed." Then she leaned in close and whispered in Bragg's ear, "Shh, I'll explain everything when we get back to my cabin."

Later, Bragg would tell herself this was when it started—the first spark of the partnership that would one day shake the Empire.

Back then, she just thought Ferro was trouble. She had no idea she'd found the perfect partner for every con she'd ever dreamed of.

And she never anticipated falling for her.

◆

At first, it was small jobs. Ferro could talk her way into restricted zones and out of consequences, and Bragg—clever, blunt, and always underestimated—had a gift for turning bad odds into opportunity. Somewhere between long nights cramped in shuttle holds and laughing their way out of situations that should've gotten them ejected into space, something unspoken began to settle between them. A brush of fingers over a shared datapad. A lingering look after a close call. A warmth that neither of them named but both felt like gravity.

It didn't take long before they pooled what little they had and bought *The Rook*, a battered old hauler with mismatched engines and a temperamental AI that refused to speak in complete sentences. It was a reckless choice, the kind people made when they realized they wanted the same future—or at least the same direction. And even if neither of them said it out loud, the moment they signed the transfer papers, Bragg knew that she hadn't just chosen a ship. She'd chosen Ferro, too.

Their small ship ran cons across the mid-systems—selling forged passage permits to desperate miners, siphoning ore from unmanned refineries, intercepting signal beacons and "returning" them for ransom. They weren't rich, but they were free—and that counted for more.

The Empire didn't care about small-timers like them, not out here. The mid-systems were the cracks between its glittering core worlds and the starving fringe, where the bureaucrats stopped watching and the patrols rarely came. Out here, you survived by your wits or not at all.

Bragg loved it—the chaos, the noise, the endless possibilities of an open starfield. Ferro loved the art of it. Every grift was a performance: new face, new accent, new lie spun out of starlight and nerve.

On long hauls between jobs, Bragg would sit on the bridge watching Ferro practice her personas in the reflection of the nav screen, shifting her posture, her voice, even the color of her eyes. Sometimes Ferro would catch her looking, and instead of switching personas, she'd soften—just enough for Bragg to see the woman beneath all the masks. On quieter nights, Ferro would curl into the crook of Bragg's arm in their narrow bunk, gossiping about marks they'd fooled or dreams they secretly held. It wasn't just comfort; it was gravity, steady and warm.

"You could make anyone believe anything," Bragg once said.

Ferro smiled without looking up. "I only ever tell people what they want to hear."

"And what do I want to hear?"

"That you're in control."

Bragg had laughed then—short, a little breathless—but the words stuck. Ferro always knew exactly which buttons to press. Exactly where Bragg's armor was thinnest.

They might have kept drifting like that forever—two women and a pair of mouthy droids, lovers moving from one small scam to the next, sleeping tangled together between the stars—if Bragg hadn't started wanting more. She'd begun studying Imperial trade routes, tracing them late at night while Ferro slept beside her. Noting how often the same freighters moved through unguarded space, how much wealth passed between worlds under the Emperor's crest... and wondering what they might claim if they aimed higher.

But even then—even wrapped in Bragg's arms, even with the stars stuttering gold and blue across the bulkhead—Ferro felt distance creeping in. A subtle shift. A gravity loss. Bragg's mind was already somewhere else.

It became sharper after their next job: a quick smash-and-switch on a drifting cargo scow carrying illegal plasma coils. Clean, simple, quiet. Ferro ran distraction with a false distress call while Bragg and the droids popped the hull seals, stole the coils, and were gone before the scow's automated systems reawakened. A tidy payday, the kind that usually had Bragg crowing all the way to the next jump.

Instead, she'd been silent. Thinking too hard.

They celebrated anyway—protocol on *The Rook* after any job that didn't include burns or funerals. Bragg set them down on Kessa-9, a rust-ridden rock with a breathable atmosphere and a single street of neon-sick businesses, all of them ways for desperate people to lose money.

They hit their favorite den—the Rusted Hound, where the air smelled like scorched synthale, wet coats, and ambition gone sour. Shady captains, smugglers with more scars than teeth, gamblers who owed favors they couldn't repay. Home, in its own crooked way.

Ferro nursed a coppery drink while Bragg shot pool against a pair of mercenaries, grinning bright and dangerous. B377Y leaned on the table, making snide commentary about everyone's form, while V3R0N1C4 calculated odds aloud until someone paid her to stop.

That was when they heard it—whispers from a ragged group of traders at the next table.

"... Vault's real, I'm telling you. Emperor keeps the *good* stuff there..."

"... coordinates nobody's seen in centuries..."

"... tech from before the starfall..."

Bragg froze mid-shot. Missed by a mile.

Ferro saw it happen: the ignition. The spark behind Bragg's eyes that meant trouble had just become destiny.

And from that night on, Bragg changed.

She spent hours on the bridge mapping the Imperial Palace. Studying the Emperor's routines. Digging through old smuggler logs. The blue light from the displays carved hollows into her cheeks; she looked lit from the inside by starlight and obsession.

Ferro felt her slipping away long before she understood why.

She confronted Bragg two nights later, when Bragg had been pacing the bridge for hours, cycling through the same star charts like she could will the constellations to rearrange in her favor.

"You're planning something," Ferro said, leaning in the doorway. "And it's not small. You think I can't tell when you're winding yourself up for a leap?"

Bragg stopped, shoulders tight. "I was going to tell you."

"You were going to let me figure it out when it was too late," Ferro shot back. "So tell me now."

Bragg exhaled, long and slow. Then she gestured her closer—not with guilt, but with the conviction of someone who believes the world will bend to her will if she just holds it hard enough.

Ferro crossed her arms and waited.

With a flick of her wrist, Bragg opened the holo-map. Imperial space bloomed red-gold across the room, stars glittering like shards of a crown.

"The Emperor's Vault," Bragg said. "That's the target."

Ferro stared. "The Emperor's what?"

"The Vault. His private hoard. His secrets. His leverage over half the core worlds."

"A myth," Ferro muttered.

Bragg grinned, slow and wicked. "All the best heists start as myths."

Ferro felt heat simmer low in her chest—the familiar mix of terror and love that Bragg always stirred. "You think you can rob the Emperor?"

"I think we can," Bragg corrected. "But it starts with you."

Ferro's eyes narrowed. "There it is. The part you didn't want to tell me."

Bragg didn't deny it.

The plan, as Bragg described it, was simple in the way all catastrophes are, at least once Ferro seduced the Emperor.

Step one: Ferro would gain access to the Emperor's private wing.

Step two: Bragg and the droids would remotely breach the Vault's firewalls from *The Rook*'s orbit, siphoning encrypted schematics to a secondary drive hidden in Ferro's jewelry.

Step three: Bragg would execute a "precision retrieval"—her term for the most dangerous part of any job.

"And how exactly am I going to get into the Emperor's private wing?" Ferro's voice was very calm.

"You're going to infiltrate the palace," Bragg said. "From the inside."

"Say it plainly, Bragg."

"You're going to marry him."

Ferro barked a laugh—sharp, incredulous. "Bragg, marrying the Emperor is not a plan. It's a death wish."

B377Y clanked into the doorway, metal hip cocked like a bored bouncer. "Am I hearing this correctly? You intend for our hostess to become Empress?"

Bragg waved her off. "Temporary Empress."

V3R0N1C4 hummed over the comm. "Statistical probability of surviving the wedding night: two point three per cent."

"Rounding generously," B377Y added.

Ferro threw her hands up. "See? Even the machines think this is insanity."

Bragg stood and cupped Ferro's face in both hands. "Listen to me. He won't kill you."

"He's killed his wives!" Ferro snapped.

"Not the recent ones," Bragg said cheerfully, holding up fingers as she counted. "Four got cryo'd. Five got mind-wiped. Six got labor-colonied. Seven got... cosmetically rearranged. Eight was sterilized and exiled—"

"This is supposed to comfort me?"

Bragg's grin faltered. Just a little. "Ferro, I never fail. And I'm not losing you. Not to him. Not to anyone."

Ferro's breath hitched. Because Bragg meant it. Bragg always meant it. The problem was that Bragg loved her with the same force she loved impossible odds—with devotion sharpened into obsession.

"When you're the Empress," Bragg said, tracing the line of Ferro's jaw, "you'll find the Vault. Get the data. The tech. The blackmail. Then we walk."

"Precision retrieval," B377Y repeated flatly. "You mean kidnapping a queen from a fortress while her husband commands a personal fleet."

"Semantics," Bragg said.

"Suicide," B377Y said.

"Romantic," Bragg corrected. "Beam her out, quick, clean, poetic."

Ferro swallowed. "And then what? We live the rest of our lives dodging Imperial assassins? That's your big dream?"

Bragg shrugged. "When we have enough, we retire."

"You mean when *you* decide we have enough." Ferro stepped back. "When does it end, Bragg?"

"When we're safe," Bragg said softly. "When we're free for real. When I can give you something better than this—" she gestured around the cramped metal corridor "—because you deserve better."

Ferro hated how her resolve wavered at that.

"You're asking me to offer myself up like a prize," she whispered. "To let a tyrant put his brand on me just so we can steal from him."

"You won't be his," Bragg said. "You're mine."

The words were possessive, reckless—and they made Ferro's pulse stutter.

Ferro stepped closer until their foreheads touched. "You're going to burn the whole galaxy down one day," she whispered.

Bragg smiled. "Only the parts that get between us."

And Ferro—against all logic, all fear, all better judgment—let herself be pulled into Bragg's arms. The holo-stars washed over them in molten color, turning their shadows into one.

For one perfect, perilous second, Ferro forgot the Emperor, the wives, the suicide mission disguised as a fairytale.

She remembered only this:

The universe was vast. Bragg was reckless.

And Ferro was hopelessly, dangerously in love.

◆

Over the next month, the plan solidified, whether Ferro liked it or not. Bragg threw herself into preparation with the fervor of a zealot—hunched over consoles, soldering identity chips, fabricating holographic seals, and rehearsing Ferro's cover story like a director polishing her lead actress.

Ferro agreed, eventually. Against her better judgment. Against the screaming warnings of every instinct she'd honed in five years of cons. Bragg had kissed her like it was victory.

And so Ferro played along.

Bragg forged the necessary identity codes and acquired invitations to get Ferro noticed at royal auctions and receptions.

Ferro played the game flawlessly—slipping through glittering rooms with an effortless grace that made onlookers gasp and courtiers whisper. Every gesture, every glance was calculated. Every flirtation, a lie.

She rose through the ranks of suitors in days.

She caught the Emperor's attention in a week.

And on the fourteenth day, a personal summons arrived—delivered by an obsidian-armored courier whose expression looked carved from stone.

Ferro would be staying in the Imperial Palace. The Emperor intended to court her formally.

The weight of the sealed invitation felt like a noose in her hand.

Later, on the bridge, she held it out to Bragg. "This is your last chance."

Bragg looked up sharply. "To what?"

"To change your mind." Ferro's voice was steady, but her pulse wasn't. "To tell me I'm more to you than just the key to your biggest score."

Bragg stepped closer, brushing a thumb over Ferro's knuckles. "Sweetheart, if there were *any* other way, I'd take it."

"You're sure?" Ferro searched her face. "Because once I step into that palace... I'm alone."

"You won't be alone." Bragg's smile was warm, bright, and utterly unshakable. "You'll have me. Always."

Ferro wished she could believe that. Truly believe it.

B377Y stomped in, arms crossed, servos whirring in irritation. "Well, if you've both finished lying to each other, we still need to discuss extraction protocols."

"Shut it, Betty," Bragg muttered.

V3R0N1C4 chimed from the overhead speaker, voice crackling with too-cheerful static. "Updated probability of the plan's success: three point one per cent. Margin of error: concerning."

"See?" B377Y said. "Even the bucket of wires thinks this is a terrible idea."

"It's an opportunity," Bragg corrected. "And we only get one."

Ferro looked down at the shimmering Imperial seal again—an invitation, a sentence, a cage disguised as privilege.

"Then I suppose we're doing this," she whispered.

Bragg pulled her into a fierce embrace. It felt like a promise. Or a goodbye. Ferro couldn't tell the difference anymore.

The Emperor's court was worse than any of Ferro's nightmares—opulent, glacial, and laced with paranoia. Every conversation shimmered with hidden meaning; every servant's glance was a possible report.

The only thing that steadied her was the voice on the encrypted comm embedded in her earring—Bragg's, confident and infuriating as ever.

"Smile, Fer. You look guilty when you don't."

"I am guilty." Ferro spoke without moving her lips.

"You're a goddess among mortals. Act like it."

"Wait, how do you know I'm not smiling?"

"I tapped into the palace surveillance."

B377Y's voice cut in. "Captain, her pulse is irregular. She's under strain."

"She's performing," Bragg would say. "Let her perform."

"Current chance of extraction success: one point eight per cent," V3R0N1C4 intoned. "I recommend adjusting expectations."

"I am adjusting them," Bragg said. "Upward."

Ferro did exactly what Bragg had trained her to do: she watched.

On her first night in the Imperial Palace—draped in silver like a newly forged weapon—she sat at the Emperor's right hand and said almost nothing. She didn't need to. The court watched her, which meant *he* watched her, which meant the game had already begun.

When the Emperor raised a toast, Ferro tilted her glass at the precise angle that made the chandelier scatter gold across her cheekbones. When he asked where she was from, she let her voice sharpen into a faint accent he couldn't place, one he spent the rest of the night trying to catalogue. When he dismissed two senators for bickering, Ferro hid a smile behind her hand, just long enough for him to catch it.

It made him laugh. The room froze. No one ever made the Emperor laugh.

By the end of the first week, she had mapped every habit he thought he concealed:

—He preferred questions that let him talk about himself.

—He liked to believe he discovered brilliance in others.

—He relaxed only when someone else appeared unthreatening.

So Ferro perfected the art of being dazzling and harmless at once.

Harmlessness, of course, was the deadliest illusion she could cast.

Within a fortnight, the Emperor called her *my star* in front of the nobles. He gifted her a gallery of glass flowers—fragile, venomous-looking things that glittered like frozen tears. He replaced the name of an orbital station with *Ferro's Smile*.

When Bragg heard that, she laughed herself breathless over the comms.

"See? I told you he'd adore you."

"He's renaming infrastructure, Bragg," Ferro hissed, pressing a hand to her forehead. "This is not normal courtship."

"And altars," Bragg said smugly, "make the best distractions."

But Ferro didn't laugh. Not then.

Because that morning, the Emperor had taken her walking through the eastern observatory—no guards, no advisors—and opened a door she wasn't supposed to see. A door made of a metal she couldn't identify, etched with a triple-sealed lattice of quantum glass that shimmered like a star caught mid-blink.

"The palace has many relics," he'd said casually, as if the room behind that door wasn't suffocating with forbidden energy. "This one is my favorite."

He didn't let her in. He didn't have to. Ferro saw enough—the power humming behind the glass, the coldness of the guards who stood there like statues carved from fear.

The Vault existed.

And if it existed, Bragg's impossible dream suddenly felt terrifyingly real.

Later that night, Bragg's voice crackled through Ferro's private channel, bright with confidence, reckless with love.

"Tomorrow we pull the data," Bragg said. "Day after, I come get you."

Ferro turned her face into the silken pillows, lowering her voice. "You promise?"

"Sweetheart," Bragg replied, "I've never broken a promise in my life."

"That's not true."

"Fine. I've never broken one that mattered."

In the background, B377Y muttered, "Define 'matters.'"

V3R0N1C4 replied, "Statistical trend suggests: not this."

Ferro closed her eyes, imagining Bragg standing at *The Rook*'s console—smirking, brilliant, doomed.

She hoped the machines were wrong.

She feared they were right.

And beneath it all, a small, traitorous part of her dared to believe they just might win.

❖

The next day went perfectly—until everything went wrong.

Ferro slipped through the Emperor's private corridors dressed in white silk and a smile that could melt alloy. Her jewelry glinted faintly in the low light—the modified earrings carrying Bragg's transmission chip, the necklace that doubled as a data siphon.

Every step had been rehearsed until even her heartbeat matched the palace rhythm.

"You're clear," Bragg murmured in her ear. "Two guards ahead, one behind. Left at the statue with the wings—good. That door. You're doing beautifully."

"Flattery from you?" Ferro whispered, lips barely moving. "I must be dying."

"Not on my watch."

Inside the Vault antechamber, the air smelled faintly of ozone and cold metal. Ferro placed her hand on the recognition plate and smiled when it burned faintly. The Emperor had already given her limited clearance—his "beloved's curiosity," he'd called it. She played the part to perfection, letting the surveillance lenses see what they wanted: devotion, reverence, awe.

"Commencing uplink," B377Y's voice cut in. "Firewall penetration at forty per cent."

"Keep going," Bragg said. "Fer, stay casual."

Ferro moved through the gallery as if she were admiring the relics—artifacts under glass, ancient weapons, sealed data cubes. The siphon necklace hummed against her collarbone, drawing down encrypted streams faster than she could breathe.

But there was something else in the room—something Bragg hadn't seen in the stolen schematics. A narrow pedestal in the far corner, bathed in faint violet light. On it rested a small black case, smooth as obsidian and marked with a single sigil: the Imperial crest, reversed.

It shouldn't have been there. And yet it was.

"Bragg," Ferro whispered. "There's something new. Not on your map."

"Ignore it."

"You always say that when it's important."

"I mean it, Fer. Stay on plan."

But Ferro had learned from Bragg too well. She slipped the small case into her sleeve as the siphon completed its cycle.

"We're good," Bragg said. "Extraction window in thirty seconds."

That was when the lights changed—from soft gold to deep crimson. The Vault's doors slammed shut. Ferro froze as alarms echoed through the marble corridors.

"Talk to me," Bragg demanded.

"I didn't—" Ferro started, but her voice was drowned by the rising wail.

The comm crackled, then cut through with a new voice. Deep. Calm. Amused.

"Captain Bragg," the Emperor said. "How lovely to finally make your acquaintance."

Ferro went still. The sound of his voice filled the chamber like gravity.

"Who?" Bragg stalled, fingers flying over her console.

"Oh, let's not play pretend," the Emperor replied. "You've been very clever, both of you. But the game ends now."

"Fer, hold on," Bragg said. "I'm pulling you out."

The beam engaged, wrapping Ferro in pale light—but it flickered, splintered, and failed. The palace shields had rerouted mid-sequence. For one heart-stopping instant, Ferro saw the stars open around her—and then nothing but darkness.

"Talia!" she screamed as the world folded back in on itself.

Bragg's signal vanished.

❖

"Ferro?" Bragg hissed. Static. She slammed her fist on the console hard enough to bruise. "B377Y, reestablish the link!"

"No signal, Captain," the robot said. "Palace defenses are cycling through our channels."

"Reroute through the beacon band!"

"Already tried it. They've locked us out."

On the holo-screen, the palace shimmered beneath its energy shell—smooth, serene, untouched. Then the sensors screamed.

"Incoming," V3R0N1C4 said flatly. "Class-seven cruiser. Imperial signature."

"They can't have traced us that fast," Bragg muttered.

"Correction," V3R0N1C4 replied. "They can and did."

The first volley hit before Bragg could curse. *The Rook* shuddered, hull plating buckling under the energy blast. Lights flickered, alarms wailed, and a thin line of smoke curled from the aft systems.

"Shields at forty per cent," B377Y said. "Recommend evasive maneuvers, or—"

"Or we die. Yes, thank you, B," Bragg snapped.

She yanked the control yoke, sending the ship spinning through the upper atmosphere. Clouds turned to streaks of molten color around them.

"We can't stay!" V3R0N1C4 said. "If we don't jump now—"

"Ferro's still down there!"

The ship rocked again. Something deep in the hull tore with a metallic scream. Bragg's hands hovered over the jump controls. For a heartbeat, she just stared at the palace on the screen—its gleaming towers, its neat little lies.

"Captain," B377Y said softly, "she would tell you to go."

Bragg's jaw locked. "I know."

And she punched the jump.

The Rook vanished into hyperspace, leaving Ferro behind.

❖

They spent the next five months chasing ghosts.

At first, Bragg attacked the search with her usual swagger—shaking down port officials, bribing data clerks, intimidating smugglers, even buying drinks for a pair of disgraced admirals who wouldn't shut up about "lost women in cold places." Every trail promised something and collapsed into nothing. Every rumor dissolved under scrutiny.

By month two, swagger was gone.

By three, Bragg had burned through half their contacts and most of her patience. *The Rook* limped from starport to starport, patched together with borrowed parts and worse luck, leaving a trail of IOUs and angry mechanics.

"We're running out of credits," V3R0N1C4 warned, for the ninth time.

"We're running out of leads," B377Y added, for the eighth.

"We're not running out of determination," Bragg snapped back, for the thirty-second.

But even she was fraying. Bragg hardly slept; when she did, she dreamed of Ferro calling her name from behind sealed doors or buried under Imperial marble. The ship felt wrong without Ferro—quieter, colder, full of empty chairs and conversations that never happened.

Once, B377Y found Bragg sitting alone in the cockpit with every sensor channel open, staring into static like she could will a signal into existence.

"You can't find her by brute force," she said.

"Watch me," Bragg muttered.

By month five, even she no longer believed her own bravado—but she refused to stop. Stopping meant Ferro was gone.

So when they finally caught the right whisper—an unregistered beacon barely strong enough to register, drifting in the periphery with a genetic signature that matched Ferro's—Bragg didn't celebrate. She froze.

"It could be bait," B377Y said gently.

"Or corrupted data," V3R0N1C4 offered.

Bragg didn't answer. Her hands were already moving, setting a course.

If it was a trick, she'd spring it. If it was a lie, she'd tear it open. If it was Ferro—

She didn't let herself finish the thought.

◆

The cryo-pod drifted among debris and ice, spinning slow and lonely in the void. B377Y handled the grappler. V3R0N1C4 initiated the thawing cycle with clinical precision.

"Still beautiful, after all this time," Bragg whispered, her fingers hovering over the console before she forced herself to press the release.

The pod hissed. Frost melted. Ferro's lashes flickered, her eyes opening as if resurfacing from a dream she hadn't chosen.

"Welcome back," Bragg said, voice soft in a way it hadn't been in months.

Ferro's first breath turned into a cough. Her voice was a rasp. "You left me."

Bragg flinched. "I had to. The ship—"

"You left me."

B377Y glanced between them. "Six months apart and still so much tension."

"Emotional confrontation detected," V3R0N1C4 added. "Should I—"

"Mute yourselves," Bragg snapped.

Ferro pushed herself upright, still trembling. "Six months in the dark, Talia. Six months."

"Technically one month with the Emperor, five in cryo—"

Ferro laughed—a raw, humorless sound. "You think that makes it better? One month in his palace felt like a lifetime. And every day I waited for you to come rescue me. Captain Bragg, breaker of walls. Savior of impossible situations. My impossible situation."

Her gaze sharpened, grief hardening. "But you didn't. Not until the danger was gone and the glory was, too."

"I searched every system in the periphery," Bragg said, her voice thin.

"After you ran."

The tension thickened—but the deck suddenly thrummed beneath them. The lights flickered.

"Unregistered mass readings," V3R0N1C4 said. "Several large signatures... surrounding us."

"Cloaked ships," B377Y whispered. "Hundreds of them."

Bragg's spine stiffened. "We need to get to the bridge. Now."

B377Y swept Ferro into her arms—not because she was helpless, but because the deck was pitching hard as *The Rook*'s inertial dampeners struggled. Bragg led the way, sprinting through the narrow corridor. Alarms wailed. The starfield outside the cargo bay viewport shimmered—and the Emperor's fleet materialized like ghosts shedding their skin.

They made the bridge just as the comm cracked open.

"Captain Bragg. Ferro. You didn't really think you'd slip past me, did you?"

His voice was almost gentle.

"I left a little sensor in your pretty pod, Ferro. A heartbeat's worth of signal—just enough to tell me when my property woke."

Ferro's hands clenched. "You bastard."

"I prefer Majesty," he said. "Prepare for boarding. I'm here for what you stole from me. I will be the one to unlock its power—not a thief and her little shapeshifter." A smile. "The black box answers to its rightful master."

Bragg went very still.

The Emperor wasn't here for vengeance.

He was here because he wanted to use the box himself.

She turned to her crew. "Battle stations. We're not running this time."

"We can't win," V3R0N1C4 said.

"Maybe not," Bragg replied, eyes burning, "but we can make him regret finding us."

Ferro staggered to a console, bracing herself. Something pulsed faintly beneath the fine scales of her collarbone. She reached beneath them and pulled free a thin opalescent necklace—its light shimmering in rhythm with *The Rook*'s systems.

"The Emperor thinks we were after the black box," she said, voice still shaking. "He took it when they caught me. Said it belonged to the old worlds, before the Gates fell." She held up the necklace. "But the siphon pulled everything from the Vault. Every secret. Every blueprint. All the new tech in the Empire."

Bragg stared. "You kept this hidden?"

"Under my skin," Ferro said simply. "Bio-conductive scales don't show on Imperial scanners."

Before Bragg could answer, the ship lurched. The comm crackled again, flooding the bridge with the Emperor's smooth, venomous voice.

"Touching reunion. You'll forgive the intrusion, but I hate to miss a sentimental moment. Bring her to me."

A tractor beam locked onto *The Rook*, dragging it toward the flagship. B377Y's hands flew over the controls, fighting the pull.

"Counter-thrust ineffective," she said. "We're being boarded."

Ferro grabbed Bragg's arm. "Don't let him take me."

Bragg's gaze locked on hers. "He'll have to kill me first."

"That can be arranged," came the Emperor's voice.

A column of blue light struck the deck. Ferro vanished—beamed away.

"Ferro!" Bragg roared. She slammed her fists into the comm. "Bring her back, you bastard!"

The Emperor's image shimmered into being above the dais—his expression almost tender.

"Did you really think you fooled me, my dear? When I chose to court you, I had Intelligence run your profile." His smile sharpened. "Your papers were flawless. Too flawless. Every record too neat, every credential just this side of believable."

Ferro's jaw tightened.

"So I asked them to dig deeper. They put your face through every database in the galaxy, ran your patterns against ten thousand unregistered colonies." His gaze flicked briefly toward Bragg. "And then your real name appeared. Along with hers."

Bragg froze.

"Yes," the Emperor said mildly. "My intelligence staff found your captain. A decorated fugitive with a remarkable talent for turning my border patrols into smoldering wreckage."

He leaned in slightly, voice softening.

"I knew then why you came to me. Not for power. Not for luxury." His eyes narrowed. "For *her*."

Ferro appeared behind him, strapped into a restraint frame.

"You, Captain Bragg, will watch as the soul is peeled from your beloved. And she will watch your ship burn."

B377Y whispered, "Captain—audio only. He can't see the lower deck feed."

Bragg leaned low, pretending to slump. "Betty. Vee. Upload everything from the necklace. Now."

"Processing," said V3R0N1C4. "Data structure... immense."

"Break it."

Schematics burst onto the hidden monitors. Warp patterns. Cloaking algorithms. Drive tech older than the Empire.

B377Y whistled. "Prototype-level. Ancient."

"Can we use it?" Bragg's voice hardened.

"It'll only take me a minute to configure." B377Y's fingers flew through the code. "Should work. Or we might explode."

"Dump everything nonessential."

"Captain," V3R0N1C4 warned, "the waste tanks contain—"

"I know what's in them. Enough DNA for a convincing explosion. Dump them."

She didn't look up. "Betty—when I say go, you beam Ferro back. Vee—prep the cloak and jump. Everything detonates behind us."

"Calculated survival probability: two point four per cent."

Bragg gave a humorless smile. "Then let's round up."

The Emperor's image flickered. "Captain Bragg, where are you hiding?"

Bragg straightened, stepping back into view. "Right here, Majesty. Just... admiring your handiwork."

He smirked. "Power you can't touch always fascinated you."

She glanced at the cables being attached to Ferro's temples, then at the black box—pulsing like a heart.

"You always wanted it used," Bragg said.

"I wanted *to* use it," he corrected. "And now I will."

"The subject is ready, Your Majesty," an Imperial tech said.

"Excellent."

B377Y's optics flashed green.

Bragg lifted her hands. "You win. Satisfied?"

"Immensely."

He turned to his crew. "Open fire. And start the de-souler."

"Only one thing wrong with your plan," Bragg said. "Ferro and I go down together. Betty—now!"

Everything exploded into motion.

Ferro vanished from the Emperor's deck in a streak of light.

The black box screamed.

The Rook dumped its cargo—a glittering cloud of debris and frozen waste.

The Rook cloaked, jumped, and was gone.

◆

Later, in a tavern on a small moon at the far edge of the mid-systems, a broadcast played to a half-interested crowd. The holo shimmered above the bar, painting everything in Imperial blue.

"—and so ends the treachery of the false queen, the hybrid Ferro of the Verryn line, and her human accomplice, the smuggler Bragg. Their ship was destroyed at the edge of the periphery. No remains recovered. The Emperor mourns their corruption, but justice has prevailed."

The announcer's voice was syrupy with reverence. The holo shifted to show the Emperor in mourning black, hand over his heart, eyes lifted heavenward.

"Let their ashes drift as warning to all who betray the throne."

The feed looped again, and the tavern filled with the low hum of conversation and clinking glasses.

At a corner table, a rough-faced pilot raised his mug. "To the women who nearly fooled the whole damn Empire," he said. "May they rest in peace—or pieces."

A ripple of laughter followed.

"I heard they just vanished," someone offered. "Gone in a flash, like ghosts."

"Nah," said another, leaning forward. "Word is the Emperor keeps them both locked in his palace. Personal favorites. Sex slaves."

A few snorted. "You believe that?"

"Why not?" came a new voice—a short, mustachioed patron at the next table, grin crooked beneath his drink. His voice had a lilting edge to it, just a shade too soft for his build. "If I were the Emperor, I'd keep them both too."

His companion, a tall Nexarian with iridescent scales covering her body, tried and failed to suppress a laugh. "You're incorrigible," she murmured, nudging his boot under the table.

He winked. "Only when I'm right."

At the next table, two service bots sat with untouched glasses. The taller one, polished chrome with violet eyes, tilted her head. "Statistically speaking," V3R0N1C4 said, "the probability of escape is less than one per cent. The sex-slave hypothesis, however, has a forty-eight per cent likelihood of being the most widely believed version."

B377Y swiveled her dome toward her. "And yet," she said, voice dripping with manufactured boredom, "here we are, drinking overpriced coolant while the 'dead' ones probably toast us from orbit."

"Speculative," said V3R0N1C4.

"Sure," B377Y said. "But speculation's how legends start."

The mustachioed patron snorted into his drink; his scaled companion's shoulders shook with silent laughter.

As the bartender locked up later that night, he stopped to admire the twin moons glimmering on the hull of a small freighter lifting from the docks—quiet, unregistered, and very much alive.

About the Author

Jessica Wilcox is from Buffalo, New York, where she lives with her husband, three children, two cats, and a dog. When she's not writing, she's an assistant principal in a local high school. She also loves reading, traveling, and practicing yoga.

A writing contest junkie for the past ten years, she most recently placed fifth in the NYC Midnight Flash Fiction Challenge, second place in the Archetype Romantasy Short Story Challenge and first in the Archetype Spooky Microfiction Challenge. She has also published fiction, nonfiction, and poetry both online and in print.

You can find a list of her publications at www.jessicaswriting space.wordpress.com/about, including links to her stories available online.

DAILY DOZEN

BY MYNA CHANG

1918

William Burelle knew death was only moments away. The flu had settled into his lungs, his heart. He barely had enough strength to reach across the bed for his wife's hand, seeking the comfort of her warmth. Meredith's stiff fingers did not respond.

He would have sobbed aloud, but he didn't have the breath for it.

Across the room, his three-year-old son, Billy, slept on a little cot. The boy stirred, cheeks pink with health. It seemed a miracle the flu had only given the boy a sniffle. But what would happen to him after both parents died? William had heard stories of the harsh Chicago orphanage, the dreadful fate that often awaited those fatherless children: neglect, freezing cold, starvation. Or worse.

"Please," William mouthed, lips moving soundlessly. "Let me… see my boy safe."

As his vision dimmed, a soothing voice came to him. "William Burelle, your allotted breath is at its end. It is time to release your burdens."

William struggled to open his aching eyes, desperate to see his little boy one last time. "Not yet," he whispered.

The voice modulated into a crystalline vibration that thrummed William's bones, chimed deep into the roots of his teeth.

"You may extend your time. But the sacrifice will be difficult for a good man."

The voice reminded William of shattered china as each word seemed to grate the cusps of his fingernails.

"How?" he whispered.

"You will receive twelve names every morning. You must choose one to take your place. One to die, so you can live another day."

William's stomach clenched. "No! I'd never choose another man's death."

The exclamation triggered a wave of wracking coughs. Blood-tinged spit stained William's lips and he gasped, lungs spasming uselessly. Little Billy woke at the ugly sound and tiptoed across the room. He placed his tiny hand on top of William's. "Please get better, Papa," he said in the soft little-boy voice that William loved so dearly.

The child leaned toward his mother's body. "Mama, wake up."

William wanted to hold the boy, protect him from the truth of his mother's fate. What kind of man would choose to abandon his child? Weakly, he nodded assent. "Just a few days. Until I find someone to care for Billy."

"Of course," the voice cut. "You may end the bargain at any time by choosing your own name."

A parchment covered in names came into William's hand. He squinted to see them more clearly, recognizing only the last name on the list. His own. He returned to the top. Nauseous shame swelled as he pronounced the first name there: Toby Hill.

His next breath flowed clear, lungs pumping smoothly. The suddenness of it robbed him of other thoughts. Breath in. Breath out. No rattling, no pain. No phlegm threatening to drown him. Another breath, deeper this time. Sweet and clean. The sandpaper grit in his eyes eased.

He blinked, seeing clearly for the first time in days. Better than clear; he hadn't seen this well since childhood. The colors took on a new vibrance, as if fresh new life flooded everything under his gaze. The faded red of the blanket surged, now a deeply textured hue. The tattered threads of the curtain's lace stood white and crisp against the windowpane. His son's hair tumbled in shades of rich chestnut.

William flexed his fingers. No longer swollen, the joints moved with delightful precision. He sat up and stretched. It felt good to move his muscles again. "Come here, sweetling," he said to Billy, thrilled at the renewed strength in his voice.

He rocked his son back to sleep and tucked him into the cot, warm and snug. Looking past the corpse of his beloved wife, he smiled.

Later, after he'd made arrangements for Meredith's body and purchased fresh bread to accompany the canned beans he intended to heat for dinner, he glanced through the afternoon newspaper. Among reports of the flu epidemic, he saw a mention of a young boy who had fallen from a third-story tenement window early that morning. According to the devastated father, little Toby Hill had inexplicably lost his balance and toppled to his death.

William froze as the name clicked into place. A child. That's why his vision had improved so drastically; he was seeing through the eyes of a child—one he himself had chosen for sacrifice. He stuffed the newspaper in the trash and strode to the bathroom mirror. His brown eyes now held a hint of green in their depths. William shuddered and looked away.

The next morning, he awoke to another list. He shoved it aside, refusing to look at it, thinking instead of green-eyed Toby Hill. Imagining that other father's grief.

"No, I can't do it," he said out loud. "I won't choose."

A familiar ache slammed into his body, and his lungs rasped, ragged and wet. Exhaustion weighed heavy with each slowing beat of his heart. William panicked at the return of searing fever, the terror of drowning in his own fluids.

Little Billy's blanket rustled as the boy turned, peacefully asleep. William keened, the whine of a miserable animal. Refusing to choose was the same as choosing himself, and William quaked in the face of death. The list trembled as he held it in his hand. Twelve names awaited him. All unfamiliar, except his name at the bottom.

His finger hovered, then pointed to the stranger's name at the top. He hoped it did not belong to another child.

His breath stuttered, then returned, steady and pure.

1930

William seethed as fifteen-year-old Billy described the incident with his boss. Jeb Yeardley owned the grocery store where Billy stocked shelves after school. The month's wages should have been enough for a new pair of shoes. Yeardley had skimped on the payment, giving Billy only half of what he was owed.

"These rich people think they can get away with murder," William ranted. "While good people like us barely scrape by."

Billy slumped into his mother's worn old chair. "I'll find another job, Papa. Right after school tomorrow."

William sighed. "I'm sorry, Billy."

The next morning, William woke with a stone in his heart. He hated for his son to walk to school another day in those worn-out oxfords. Frowning, he grabbed the daily list and scanned the names, recognizing several from the news: a bigshot actor, a couple of government officials. William stopped when he saw Jeb Yeardley on the list. What kind of man cheats a hard-working boy? William had never before chosen someone he knew personally. He smiled as he selected the greedy grocery store owner for the day's sacrifice.

The wave of energy that hit him was stronger than usual, leaving him not only invigorated, but also *satisfied*. Instead of the pang of guilt that often accompanied his choice, this time, William swelled with pride. He'd made the world a better place—a safer place—for good boys like his Billy.

He chuckled as he dressed, then sobered when he saw his son's ratty shoes in a heap by the door. He sighed and bent down to retrieve the emergency savings he kept in an old cigar box under his bed. William savored the lingering aroma of tobacco as he opened the lid, expecting to find ten dollars in spare change. He stared at the contents of the box, then let out a jubilant *whoop* as he counted out three hundred dollars in neatly folded bills.

This little bite of Yeardley's grocery fortune convinced William that he had, indeed, made the right choice.

The next morning, on the line above William's name, *Billy Burelle* appeared on the list.

1944

As always, William scanned the list for people that would give him a sense of righteousness when he condemned them. Maybe a thief. A doctor accused of malpractice. That hussy who worked nights at the diner. What kind of woman would leave her children alone at night? Sometimes the names were foreign-sounding. He didn't hesitate to choose those. Who knew what kind of godless people they might be?

But some days, there would be a celebrity on this list. Someone known for their wealth, their grace and charm. Their youth. Some trait that William wanted to claim for his own. He perused the list, hoping to find something well suited for the special day ahead. Ah, there. That new singer from the supper club. Such a resonant voice.

William sang a half-remembered hymn as he showered, appreciating the enhanced timbre of his voice in the steamy bathroom. When the hot water began to cool, he stepped out of the shower and pulled on a thick bath robe. He examined his face in the mirror, noting the rich color in his beard: his customary brown, infused with a deep chocolate-red. The hair was thick and soft to the touch, and William frowned as he reached for the peroxide. It was a shame to diminish his lush good looks, but he couldn't continue to appear so young in public, especially now that his first grandson had arrived.

He hummed a lullaby as he headed out the door, eager to hold little William Burelle III.

1962

William admired his new bedroom, sparkling with California sunshine. Of course, he'd have to get used to the new name. William Allson. The change grated, but the new identity allowed him to shake off the burden of pretending to be elderly.

His heart had almost cracked as he'd watched Billy and the grandchildren weeping at his funeral. But it also gratified him. He'd sacrificed so much for their wellbeing over these long years. It was good to know they appreciated him.

He luxuriated in the slide of his supple skin on silk sheets as he considered the daily list. In addition to his and Billy's names, he saw the names of his three oldest grandchildren. He scowled at the inclusion of *William Burelle III*. He skimmed past his family, choosing instead the uppity secretary from the Beverly Hills motor vehicle office. She had given him such a hard time over the discrepancy on his birth certificate.

He could almost taste the surge of energy, alighting on his tongue like a fine sparkling wine.

1979

The scent of sizzling bacon wafted from the open balcony doors. His young wife was an excellent cook. He quickly made his selection from the daily dozen list and hurried down to breakfast on the verandah. He kissed her cheek and sat while she served his coffee.

A newspaper waited, open to the obituary page. William never looked at the obits anymore; it was more pleasant to avoid the names of people he had known—and the people he had doomed.

"Did you put this here?" he asked his new Meredith.

"No," she answered. "I assumed you did."

He glanced at the page and his heart squeezed. *Billy Burelle, deceased.*

William slumped, remembering the soft texture of his baby's hair, hearing again the sweet lilt of his voice. His precious little boy, dead and gone.

How had he not noticed the absence of Billy's name on the daily list? William stared into the crystal sky, wondering when he'd lost track of his son, musing that, perhaps, it was time to stop. Time to release his burdens and join his beloved Billy in the afterlife.

Meredith joined him at the table, interrupting his thoughts. "Sweetheart, I have something to tell you," she said with a shy smile. "How do you feel about becoming a father?"

William's forehead wrinkled in surprise. Then he laughed. What kind of man would abandon his wife and unborn child? He hugged her tight.

The next morning, for the first time ever, William's name was not on the list. But he knew the name of every other person there. His grandchildren. The great-grandkids, too. Each one bore the Burelle name, except one: *William Allson, Junior* topped the list.

William's finger hovered, quivering as he considered his daily choice.

About the Author

Myna Chang (she/her) is the author of The Potential of Radio and Rain *(CutBank Books). Her writing has been selected for W.W. Norton's* Flash Fiction America, Best Small Fictions, *and* Best Microfiction. *She is the winner of the Lascaux Prize in creative nonfiction and the New Millennium Writing Award for flash. Her speculative short stories have been included in the Locus Recommended Reading List and longlisted for the British Science Fiction Association award; her poetry has received an honorable mention in the* Science Fiction & Fantasy *Poetry Association's Rhysling Awards, and featured in the* 2025 Worldcon Souvenir Program Book. *She hosts the* Electric Sheep *speculative reading series and publishes* MicroVerse Recommended Reading. *She lives in Maryland, USA.*

Find her at MynaChang.com and on Bluesky at @MynaChang.

GOOD MANNERS

BY PATSY PRATT-HERZOG

The child was afraid, and it was all my fault. I could hear her terrified weeping even over the raging storm.

I sank my claws into the deck as the ship heaved beneath me, pushing us skyward. The scent of ozone and brine was heavy in the air, offending my sensitive nose. The mackerel I'd had for breakfast threatened to make a reappearance as we rolled over the crest of the wave and dropped off the other side. The process repeated in seemingly endless succession as the storm raged on, tossing *The Poisoned Rose* from wave to wave like a child's toy. The ship groaned and creaked around me as if it were in physical pain, and I yowled in agreement. The weather on this benighted planet was far too turbulent. I'd take space travel any day over this primitive mode of water voyaging.

So, what was a space-faring feline like me doing on a pirate ship, one might reasonably ask? I was hunting a feral outlaw.

Nova Jinx was a smuggler and a thief, and she'd really ruffled some fur this time. Before she left for Earth, she'd robbed the Galactic History Museum, and the Clan Chiefs had put a price on her head big enough to tempt even me. I'd been chasing her around this planet for weeks. Now, she was running with a crew of human pirates in what Earthlings called the Caribbean Sea.

I was bringing her in if it was the last thing I ever did… and with things going the way they were… that was a distinct possibility.

I let out a plaintive mew as the ship rolled over another wave, and Dinah looked down at me from the Captain's bunk, her brown eyes large and tearful.

"Make it stop, Finn," she begged.

I touched the child's thoughts, sending as much calm and comfort as I could manage. It was the least I could do. Her mother was up top, trying to steer us through this tempest.

I had made a "suggestion" to Captain Delahaye that she set sail for Port Royal despite her resistance to the idea. I should have paid more attention to her troubled thoughts about a change in the wind, but Nova was there, and my single-minded focus had gotten us all into trouble.

Technically, after that debacle in Ancient Egypt where Bastet had set herself up as a deity to be worshiped, the ruling council had forbidden us to show our power or use it to influence inferior beings, but my soldiering days were over. I was a bounty hunter now, and my interpretation of the rules was a bit more... flexible.

Bastet had been the most powerful ever among our kind, both telepathically and telekinetically. Legend had it she'd created a jeweled collar that amplified her natural abilities. I had nothing near the juice she'd possessed, but I was at the higher end of the scale. Controlling weather had never really been my thing, but if it kept me from getting my paws wet, I was damned well going to try.

Sinking my claws into the floorboards with every step, I made my way across the pitching deck of the Captain's cabin to the row of windows at the back. I had no hope of calming the raging waters—the sea was too big and powerful—but maybe I could do something about the storm driving the waves. Anchoring myself before the window, I reached out to the clouds and wind, feeling for the edges of the storm. It was a great, spinning construct with an eye of calm at its center. I pushed my thoughts into that center of calm, grabbing hold of it and forcing it wider, expanding it, pushing at it with everything inside me. My center of calm ate away at the turbulence surrounding it, growing wider, drinking the storm down as it went. Panting and dizzy, I pushed more energy into enlarging this circle of calm until it washed over the ship. I kept pushing harder and further until I had nothing left to give, and the world went black around me.

◆

Consciousness drifted back to me slowly on the wings of a thrumming headache. I was held against something warm, and someone was rubbing my ears.

"Finn? Can you hear me, *mon beau minou?*"

I let out an answering mew and opened my eyes. I was still in the Captain's cabin, but the sea was blissfully calm, and I could see land through the windows. *Land! Thank the Maker!*

Captain Jacquotte Delahaye held my considerable bulk in her arms as if I were a human child. Her long, red hair was still damp from the storm, but she was smiling. I'd always found her to be surprisingly good-natured for a pirate.

With my large paws and tufted ears, I more closely resembled a dark-furred lynx than a domestic tabby. Add in intense blue eyes and a long, prehensile tail, and I had given even Jacquotte pause when we first met, but I'd quickly won her over with my charming personality.

"There's my pretty boy." She kissed me on the head, and I purred for her as she scratched between my ears. The sound and feel of a purring feline seemed to put humans in a pliant mood.

If the Clans ever decided to conquer Earth, it would be ridiculously easy, I mused. Through careful experimentation, I'd discovered humans would do almost anything for you if you purred loud enough.

"What happened, Dinah?" Jacquotte asked her daughter. "Did something fall and hit Finn?"

Dinah was looking at me with far more acumen than a six-year-old child should possess. "No, Maman. He got shiny, and then he fell down."

Perceptive little minx.

"Shiny?" Jacquotte asked. "Do you mean his eyes? Cats have special eyes that shine in the dark."

"No, Maman," the child said, shaking her head. "All of him was shiny like the moon, and then the wind stopped blowing, and he fell down."

Laughing, Jacquotte sat me on the bed and reached for her daughter. "Perhaps it is your head I should be looking at, *mon Coeur*," she said, poking playfully through the child's red curls.

"No," Dinah insisted. "Finn is special, Maman."

Perceptive and intelligent. I looked into the child's wide brown eyes with newfound respect. I would have to be more careful around her.

Captain Delahaye stroked my head. "It is good to have a special kitty. He goes well with all our other treasures."

"Is that why we are here, Maman?" Dinah asked. "For treasure?"

Jacquotte frowned, confusion swimming in her dark eyes. "I... I came for something, though now I am not sure what. Perhaps your maman also needs her head looked at?"

Dinah giggled.

"Would you like to see your *papa, mon Coeur*?" Jacquotte asked. "I noticed *The Satisfaction* is in port."

Dinah bounced up and down excitedly. "Can we go now?"

I wanted to bounce with her. Nova was last seen on Henry Morgan's flagship. I very much wanted to pay Dinah's papa a visit.

❖

The sea was blissfully calm, and a light breeze ruffled my fur with gentle fingers as I stood at the bow of the longboat. Captain Delahaye's men rowed us toward *The Satisfaction*. She was at anchor, and her sails were down. For a primitive wooden vessel, the triple-masted frigate was pleasing to the eye. Her upper decks were painted in three broad bands of color: red, blue, and white. She looked like a jolly ship to be so feared, but her captain was a ruthless pirate with little sympathy for those he robbed and plundered.

I looked at Dinah with her sweet disposition and innocent smile and wondered how a cold bastard like Henry Morgan had fathered such a delightful child.

I shook my head. It wouldn't do to get attached. Once my mission was complete, I'd likely never return to this planet, and the end was drawing near.

Dinah's happy smile faded, and she leaned down and hugged me tight, but I squirmed out of her embrace and leaped to the front of our boat.

I could feel Nova Jinx on that ship, and she wasn't getting away from me this time. We pulled alongside *The Satisfaction*, and I swarmed up the net and over the rail. My roving gaze caught the tip of Nova's black-ringed tail as she bolted below decks. Morgan's crew of hardened pirates scattered before me with startled curses as I ran after her.

I pursued Nova into the bowels of the ship, where she disappeared among the powder kegs and crates of supplies. When I reached the bottom of the stairs, a blast of enticing fragrance nearly knocked me off my paws.

Though it languished in an unpopulated corner of the galaxy, this backwater planet had one undeniable attraction: *Nepeta cataria*, more commonly known around these parts as catnip. The stuff was worth its weight in gold back home. Free for the picking, catnip grew wild all over this planet. Smugglers couldn't resist an easy haul like that, and Nova was no exception, but I couldn't see her expending this much effort for a few hundred pounds of Nip. I was willing to bet she was up to her whiskers in something bigger than drug running. If she had this much contraband stored up, what was she still doing here? I hadn't been able to locate her landing craft, but I was betting it was close by. Why hadn't she taken her stash and left?

I opened my mind while I could still concentrate. "Give it up, Nova."

Her thoughts roiled back to me on a wave of anger. "Fat chance, bounty hunter."

My ears perked. Over the sounds of creeping vermin, I could hear Nova scratching and clawing at something. Was she trying to dig her way through the side of the ship? I crept toward the sound.

"Why make it hard on yourself?" I asked. "Just come back with me and face the charges."

Something heavy crashed to the ground, and I hurried forward. Nova had tipped a painted box onto the floor. A bandage-wrapped bundle lay between her paws, and she was tearing at it with her teeth and claws.

My heart convulsed as I realized what the bundle was. It was a cat mummy. Surely it couldn't be...

With a cry of triumph, she stood, a gold, jewel-encrusted collar clutched in one paw.

"Weeks of manipulating pirates and raiding treasure ships, but it was all worth it for them to bring me this!" She slipped the collar over her head.

Great spluttering hairballs!

Nova's black-and-white dappled fur lit up like her namesake, and a wave of psychic energy blasted through the hold, sending rats scurrying in all directions.

I stared down at the decimated mummy of Bastet in horror, her collar of power now in Nova's clutches. This was bad. *This is very, very bad.*

Her gaze went to the corpse. "I would have preferred to treat our ancestor with more dignity, but you left me little choice."

"There's always a choice," I said, backing slowly away from her. "For example... not killing me would be a great choice."

She gave me a purring laugh. "That's a choice I'm unwilling to make."

Her green eyes blazed, and the deck started to quake beneath my paws. Several crates rose into the air and hurtled in my direction. I leaped away, hiding behind a row of power kegs as they smashed into the deck where I'd been standing.

"Now, who's prolonging things?" Nova demanded.

As she stalked me, I stayed a few steps ahead of her, keeping boxes and bins between us. I could feel her presence like a white-hot beacon in the room. I had to get that collar off her, or I was one dead kitty.

Small footsteps sounded behind me. *I know those footsteps.* I looked up in horror to see Dinah coming down the stairs.

The child is far too inquisitive for her own damned good!

"Finn?" she called.

"The first of my slaves," Nova purred.

I hissed, my ears flattening. "Leave her alone."

Nova let out a growling laugh. "The hardened bounty hunter cares for this pathetic human kitten?"

Dinah shrieked as her feet left the floor. Arms flailing, the child careened around the room, dangling upside down in the matrix of Nova's power.

"Stop!" I hissed.

"Come bow before me, and maybe I won't smash her," Nova taunted, bringing the child inches from crashing into walls and pillars as she jerked her small body this way and that.

"Help me, Finn!" Dinah screamed.

I paced around the hold, trying to keep Dinah in view as the helpless child screamed my name. I had to do something! But what? If I gave myself up, Nova would kill her anyway, just to spite me.

My head spun as I crossed into the far corner of the hold, making concentration difficult. The crates all around me were filled with

Nova's mind-altering contraband. I stopped in my tracks. *The Nip!* It was my only chance.

Reaching out to the nearest crate, I captured it in the matrix of my power. Then, pumping as much energy as possible into the force surrounding it, I hurled it at Nova like a cannon shot. It exploded around her, showering her with dried Nip. She gasped in an involuntary lungful, and her green eyes dilated wide. Then, with a blissful meow, Nova dropped to the ground and started rolling around in the spilled Nip.

Released from Nova's grasp, Dinah plummeted, screaming toward the deck. I caught her before she crashed and set her gently on her feet. Her brown eyes filled with tears as she ran to me and threw her arms around me.

"Daddy has a bad kitty," she said, hugging me tightly. I rubbed my cheek against hers, soothing her with my purr.

You have no idea how bad that kitty is, I mused, looking at the blissfully drugged-out Nova as she rolled languidly on the ground, her dark fur speckled with bits of green.

Dinah pulled back to look at me. "I know how bad she is. She's very, very bad."

I looked up at her in surprise. *Can you hear me, Dinah?*

She nodded.

Have you always been able to hear me?

She nodded again, red curls bouncing. "Yes."

The child must have had rudimentary psychic abilities.

She hugged me tightly. "You're going away now, aren't you?" she whispered into my fur.

Yes. I must take the bad kitty away so she can't hurt you again.

"Will you come back?" the child asked in a tremulous voice.

Would you like me to? I asked.

"Oh yes, Finn."

Then I will.

She drew back and gave me a gap-toothed grin.

I turned my attention to Nova, who was now snoring in a drugged haze. One thing was for sure: I couldn't go into that pile of Nip, or I'd be in the same state as Nova.

Do you see the pretty collar on the bad kitty, Dinah? I asked, and she nodded. Will you get it for me?

She hopped up and pulled the collar from around Nova's neck. Then, with Dinah's help, I got Nova boxed up in a half-filled crate of her own stash, where she should be blissfully happy for the return voyage to my ship.

Dinah picked up Bastet's Collar and held it up to the light—fractured rainbows danced and glimmered on the walls in a mesmerizing display.

"A shiny necklace for my shiny kitty," she said. Then, with a giggle, she dropped the collar over my head.

I staggered, feeling as if someone had plugged my tail into an energy socket. Power zipped through me, making my whiskers twitch and my eyes spin. I could hear the thoughts of every pirate on the ship... of every person in Port Royal! I had so much juice running through me that I could have easily lifted the entire boat out of the water and flown it around the island like a strange, wingless bird. It was a rush like nothing I'd felt before.

"Pretty!" Dinah clapped as pulses of light from my glowing fur cast dancing shadows around the hold.

The heavy collar settled around my neck like it was made for me. It was a shame I'd have to turn it in... or did I? The Clans would just put it in a dusty museum for someone like Nova to steal. As a bounty hunter, I could put it to good use.

"Do you like my present, Finn?" Dinah asked, rubbing my ears.

Whiskers twitching, I gave her a feline grin. *I love it, Dinah.* Bastet's Collar was one bit of contraband I was keeping for myself.

After all, one should never refuse a gift. It was only good manners.

About the Author

Patsy Pratt-Herzog is an emerging freelance writer from Southwestern Ohio. Her favorite genres to write are sci-fi and fantasy. She lives in the burbs with her husband, Tim, and a chunky cat named Buddy. When she's not writing, she enjoys painting and riding roller coasters.

To learn more about Patsy and see other samples of her work, you can visit her blog at patsyprattherzog.wordpress.com/featured-publications/

A Safe Place

by Faye Upton

I watched through the green lenses of my tactical binoculars as the Amazon omnicopter whirred over the boundary of the veterans' suburb, clutching a cardboard carton in its claws.

The drone jinked sideways around a chimney, made a looping detour around a utility pole, and engaged in an airborne two-step with another delivery copter heading empty-handed back to the depot.

It soared closer, closer, over picket fences and box hedges, around flagpoles and satellite dishes, and pivoted a sharp right down Victory Boulevard.

"Come on, come on," I muttered, jamming the binoculars into my eye sockets.

The omnicopter buzzed along the margin of Major Armstrong's two-story next door. I held my breath.

Twenty meters. Ten. Five—

A gust of wind blew the omnicopter sideways. Its motors whined to compensate. Too late. It tilted sideways, pirouetting like a ballerina... and crossed the Major's boundary.

The sentry guns rose from hidden panels in the manicured lawn, their barrels swiveling like pitiless eyes, their targeting lasers speckling the aerial intruder with crimson dots.

The omnicopter jerked as bullets peppered its blades. It howled, a terrible death shriek, and spiraled earthwards before crashing into the Major's ornamental birdbath.

I watched, wincing, as the Amazon parcel, with its precious contents, tumbled clear of the smoking drone.

And then, even as the sentry guns retracted smoothly into the lawn, a hatch slid open in the Major's house. A caterpillar-tracked ButlerBot robot trundled out, pincers outstretched to snatch the fallen package. As it reversed course to retreat into the house, its voice announced, in a British accent, "Parcel retrieved. Returning to Safe Place."

I slammed down the binoculars. "*Darn!*"

The Major was away, attending a regimental reunion on Mars. He wouldn't be back for a week. My husband, Chuck, and I had been anxiously awaiting that parcel. We couldn't wait. We needed it *today*.

I had to retrieve it, at any cost.

The recently installed *UltraSecure 3000* defense system panel on the outside of the Major's house seemed to taunt me.

It was time to get the squad back together.

They arrived as I was prepping a week's worth of Sam's school lunches, vacuum-sealing each bologna-and-mayo-on-white into a perfect fifteen-centimeter square. Sam liked to joke that you could practically bounce a quarter off his sandwiches. I didn't think it was funny. I took pride in the fact that there was no "practically" about it.

Corporal Dutch got here first, bearing his toolkit, the plasma pistol he'd taken as a trophy from a Jovian officer on the Ganymede campaign, and a basket of mini muffins. "Does that still work?" I asked as I set the muffins out on the best china.

"Don't know," he admitted, hefting the pistol in his frosting-smeared hand. "But you said the Major has the *UltraSecure*

3000. Projectiles ain't gonna make a dent in that kind of hardware."

"You've read up on it?" I asked.

"You bet I have."

Privates Ramirez and Anderson arrived at the same time. Ramirez had always defied the conventional stereotypes of a Galactic Marine. Even out of power armor, our skinny little redhead had a throwing arm like a trebuchet. But lobbing ordnance was always Ramirez's last resort. She came with her laptop under her arm, a weapon more deadly in her hands than a dozen frag grenades. "Can't stay long," she announced. "My *Realm of Wizardry* clan has a raid!"

Anderson squeezed through the front door behind her, the breadth of his shoulders not the impediment so much as the sizeable crate he'd brought with him. "Sorry we're late, Sergeant."

"It's fine, Private. But now you're all here—"

"It's just that Cream Puff didn't want to come to Mommy." Anderson poked an affectionate finger through the bars of the cage. "Did you, Puffy?"

"You for real?" Ramirez asked, peering at the crate from behind her laptop.

"She's my best girl," Anderson said, bristling.

"'Cream Puff'?" said Ramirez.

"'Realm of Wizardry'?" Anderson fired back.

"That's enough, Marines," I said. "We don't trash-talk each other's CLAP."

"But—"

"Have a muffin," Dutch suggested from where he'd been dismantling my Roomba. "They're lemon-blueberry."

After a moment, first Ramirez, then Anderson, grudgingly took a muffin. Not for the first time, I wondered if CLAP—the Civilian Life Adjustment Program—was really such a great idea. Along with embedding the desire for a return to civilized domestic life into servicemen and women who'd been at intergalactic war for a decade, CLAP imprinted every retired soldier with a burning passion for a particular hobby, individually selected for optimal compatibility. It was meant to give them an outlet for their military focus and intensity, but some veterans took their newfound obsessions a little *too* far. Whatever eggheads had designed CLAP hadn't counted on how some Marines would fixate on macrame, or ice sculpture, or ferret-racing—or how personally they'd take any slight to their assigned pursuit. Even one as oddball as Anderson's.

I spread a blueprint of the Major's house on the coffee table, pinning down the corners with teacups. The squad gathered round to study it.

"Jeez-Louise," whistled Anderson. "Look at that square footage?"

"Corner plot," Ramirez agreed. "Two-and-a-half baths. *Turret.*"

"Is that a *walk-in pantry*?" Dutch asked with incredulous envy.

I traced the Major's boundary with my finger. "The sentry guns cover every square centimeter of the grounds to a height of twelve meters. Anything that puts one toe into the yard is going to get a faceful of lead."

"Sheesh," said Anderson. "What if a dog goes potty on the lawn?"

"That hasn't happened since the incident with Captain Martin's Pomeranian."

"Awww," said Dutch.

"Poor puppy," said Ramirez.

I tapped the small windowless vault at the center of the schematic. "Once we're inside, the package is here, in the Major's Safe Place. Your standard panic room. Twenty-centimeter steel walls, DNA-encoded entry. And then there's the Major's ButlerBot."

"A ButlerBot?" asked Ramirez. "What's it gonna do, iron a newspaper at us?"

I shook my head. "It's an Alfred model."

"Oh. Shoot."

"Ain't you forgetting something?" asked Dutch. He tapped the front door. "Point of entry here's mag-locked with insta-kill response for Identify-Friend-Or-Foe negatives. How we gonna get inside?"

I cracked a grin. "Why'd you think I had Anderson bring the bird?"

❖

I took a final glance through the binoculars, then handed them to Anderson. He peered down them through Sam's bedroom window. "You're sure it's safe?"

"Look at the birdbath," I said. A flock of sparrows hopped and pecked around it, untroubled by the sentry guns. "The defenses won't trigger for anything under three kilos."

"Alright," Anderson said. He opened the crate. "Come on out, Cream Puff."

Cream Puff was a pigeon. Specifically, a large and fancy pigeon, with apricot plumage and an extravagant feathered crest. Anderson held her still while Dutch fastened the nanotube smart-line from his toolkit to the ring on her leg.

Ramirez squinted through the window. She took one step back, wound up, then pitched with her trademark lethal accuracy.

The lemon-blueberry muffin hit the roof of the Major's turret, bounced once, then lodged in the gutter.

Ramirez pumped her fist. "*Yes!*"

"You're up, Anderson," I said.

Anderson planted a kiss on Cream Puff's beak. "Don't let us down, Puffy-baby!"

He tossed the pigeon through the window. As Cream Puff opened her wings and dived straight for the tempting target of the muffin, the lightweight wire attached to her leg hissed off the spool in Dutch's hands.

As Cream Puff circled to land, the smart-line wrapped around the turret's apex spike. I triggered the remote release. The line detached from Cream Puff's leg and snapped three times tightly around the spike. The fine wire glimmered blue as its smart nanites activated to secure it—and then expanded into a rope that went taut in Dutch's hands.

"Lock it off, Marine!" I shouted.

Dutch snapped the spool end of the rope to the ring he'd sunk into Sam's bedroom wall.

"Synchronize comms!" I said, tapping my earpiece.

The squad followed suit. Ramirez, her fingers flying over the keys of the laptop she had open on Sam's bed, said, "No one better let their fanny dangle on the way over. You only got clearance of oh-point-nine meters between the line and the top of the sensor field!"

"Acknowledged," said Anderson. He swung himself out the window, wrapped his legs over the top of the rope, and hauled himself hand-over-hand along it with lightning speed. Dutch hitched up his backpack and followed.

I brought up the rear. As I commando-crawled along the rope, fifteen meters above the ground, I looked down. Our back lawn looked a little scruffy. I made a mental note to get Chuck to mow on Sunday.

By the time I'd crossed from Sam's bedroom window to the Major's turret, Dutch had already climbed down onto the roof. Anderson was still clinging to the shingles with one hand, trying to grab Cream Puff with the other. "Private!" I barked. "Get your head in the game!"

"Just... have to..." Anderson swiped at Cream Puff. She fluttered just out of his reach, a chunk of muffin in her beak. "Puffy... come... here!"

"Sergeant!" Dutch shouted from below.

He'd lowered himself from the roof down onto the porch without tripping the sensors. I left Anderson chasing his pigeon and shimmied down after Dutch. "We're at the insertion point, Ramirez. Proceed with phase two."

"Acknowledged," Ramirez's voice said over the comm. "Patching into the home defense grid now."

Dutch peered up at where two rotary miniguns flanked the black lens of a surveillance camera above the door. "Some *home* defense grid—"

As he shifted to examine the hardware, his foot brushed the edge of the doormat. The camera swiveled abruptly to focus on us, blinking with an ominous red light. The servos in the miniguns began to spin up with a slow whine. "INTRUDER DETECT-ED."

"Ah, shoot," Dutch swore, jerking back his foot.

"I-F-F NEGATIVE," the defense system droned. "TRESPASS IS PUNISHABLE BY DEADLY FORCE. LEAVE IMMEDI-ATELY. YOU HAVE FIVE SECONDS TO COMPLY. FIVE…"

"Pick it up, Ramirez!" I shouted.

"OK, Sergeant, I'm nearly there—"

"FOUR…"

"Sergeant!" Dutch yelled. "You're gonna need this!" He thrust a green, enameled watering can into my hands

"THREE…"

Dutch pulled a plastic misting bottle out of the pack, brandishing it at the camera like a weapon.

"Come on, come on!" I shouted.

Ramirez's voice was muffled on the earpiece. "Nearly there…"

"TWO…"

I tightened my fingers on the watering can.

"I'm in!" Ramirez cried.

The blinking red light went green. The miniguns drooped, powering down. With a *chunk*, the mag-locks released and the heavy door swung open. "HOUSEPLANT PROTOCOL EN-GAGED," said the defense system in an altogether calmer tone.

"THE SUNROOM IS DOWN THE HALL. PLEASE DO NOT OVERWATER THE ORCHIDS."

"Orchids," said Dutch. "Guess the brass get the fancy CLAPs as well as the fancy houses."

I glanced around as I tapped my earpiece. The Major's house wasn't *so* different from mine, though I'd have died for his sprung hardwood floors. I quickstepped down the hall toward the Safe Place. Dutch followed my lead. "Ramirez. What's the status of the ButlerBot?"

No response.

"Ramirez?"

Still nothing.

"Gosh-*darnit*," I muttered.

The Safe Place door was exactly as expected: a massive steel slab with a hand-scanner, and a smaller hatch for the ButlerBot. I took care not to touch anything. "Dutch, you're up!"

Dutch had already unslung his backpack. He unzipped it and removed my Roomba, reassembled and modified with grabbing arms and a spoofing field that would convince the Safe Place's software to let it in. Dutch set the Roomba on its wheels and turned it on.

And then his eyes fell on the doorway opposite the steel vault. He rose from his crouch.

"Dutch?"

He stopped in the doorway, transfixed.

"Dutch!" I barked.

"He has two ovens," Dutch said, awestruck. Then he caught his breath, his eyes going round with wonder. "And the units... they ain't... they can't have... *granite counter-tops?*"

"*Corporal Dutch!*"

"The pastry I could make in this kitchen," he whispered.

Too late, I heard the rumble of caterpillar tracks.

"Dear me; you're not supposed to be here," said a plummy voice. "Please stand quite still while I disintegrate you."

I ducked just in time to dodge the laser bolt that streaked from the ButlerBot's shoulder-mounted blaster.

"Sergeant!" Dutch pulled the plasma pistol from its holster and aimed it at the ButlerBot. He squeezed the trigger. Nothing happened. He squeezed it again, and the pistol made an embarrassed little *fzzt*. "Darn it!" He threw the pistol at the ButlerBot. It clanged harmlessly off the robot's armored chassis.

My earpiece crackled. "Sorry, sorry, sorry!" Ramirez said over the comm. "Raid started early. My cleric-mage got into a tight spot. What'd I miss?"

The ButlerBot fired again. I felt a laser bolt singe my ear on its way to making a crater in the drywall. "Perhaps you misheard me," said the ButlerBot, politely regretful. "My employer requires me to terminate you."

"Ramirez!" I shouted. "The Roomba!"

"On it!"

The Roomba slammed into the ButlerBot. Its pincers locked with the ButlerBot's arms in a near-perfect ballroom hold. The two robots spun one way, then the other, in their deadly waltz, servos whining. "My goodness," said the ButlerBot. "You are strong, Madam."

But, inexorably, the superior strength of the ButlerBot overcame the jury-rigged Roomba. With a tortured shriek, the Roomba's arms began to bend.

Then the plasma pistol suddenly pinged. "Charge complete," it announced in an incongruously cheerful voice. "Fire when ready."

I seized it and pulled the trigger.

The expanding ball of superheated plasma that erupted from the muzzle of the pistol vaporized the ButlerBot's head clean off.

The miniature artificial sun melted a meter-wide hole in the steel vault door in under a millisecond, burned through the opposite wall and, almost as an afterthought, set the Major's orchid-filled sunroom on fire.

It was dark when Chuck got in from work, shaking his head. "What the heck's been going on next door?"

"Next door, honey?" I asked, not looking up from my rapt admiration of the package sitting on the kitchen table.

"It's like a bomb hit it," said Chuck. "Two police cruisers, three fire trucks—and there was someone stuck on the roof."

That gave me a jolt. I'd totally forgotten about Anderson and Cream Puff. "I guess the Major's home defense system was on the fritz."

"Hey," said Chuck, putting his briefcase down and coming to the table. "Is that what I think it is?"

I pushed the Amazon parcel—the box only slightly scorched from its brush with the plasma pistol—across the table. "Sure is!"

Chuck's face—the craggy, severe drill sergeant visage that had been the bane of so many raw recruits—lit up with golden sparkles as he lifted out the package's glittery contents with breathless, reverent care.

Our custom-made matching samba costumes—mine, a feathered leotard; his, a sequined onesie—were beyond perfection.

Chuck hugged his jumpsuit euphorically to his chest, quivering with the anticipation of all the *botafogos* and *batucadas* it would endow with extra-spangly exuberance. "Look out, All-State Ballroom and Latin Championships 2040, because *here we come!*"

About the Author

Faye Upton is a speculative fiction writer by choice and a regular competitor and semi-regular finalist in NYC Midnight challenges. Faye is also the lead creator of Dragonchoice, *a gargantuan collaborative fanfiction and fanart project spanning twenty-five years, a million-word trilogy of novels, and an online choose-your-own-adventure game.*

She lives in Kent, near London, England, with her silver tabby Raylan. She builds websites for a living. She can't resist a rock musician and once told David Bowie he was rubbish (to his face). Her name can be found on the liner notes of his 2000 live album.
Website: www.dragonchoice.com
Email: feedback@dragonchoice.com
Facebook: snarkmaiden
BlueSky: @strictlydancers.bsky.social

HONOR, THIEVES, ETC.

BY TREY DOWELL

In the last ten years, I've seen a lot of frightening things.

The blue-and-red flashers of a cop car in the rearview mirror.
A 9x9 concrete cell.

My little brother's face when he learned I was a scumbag criminal.

All terrifying.

But nothing—repeat, nothing—scares the shit out of me more than a big pile of money sitting in the middle of a table.

When the table is surrounded by five thieves.

◈

The job had started off like most: Vance promising a huge payday, minimal work, and almost no risk. As usual, my questions mainly revolved around his definition of the words "huge" and "almost." Past experience had taught me neither word was likely to be as rosy as Vance forecasted, but a job was a job, and I'd made out alright the last couple of times he'd floated work my way. Having a former MMA fighter on the crew was a safety blanket Vance liked—just in case things went sideways. Which things frequently did.

So, I'd stolen some stuff, smacked around a couple of assholes who owed, and been the designated tough guy standing in the back of the room while a deal happened. Not exactly mastermind-level stuff, but a grand here, a grand there, had helped make ends meet, plus it'd established me as that rarest of street-level commodities: reliable muscle.

Then Vance had come calling with next-level shit. Armored car. Quarter-million on the low end. Split five ways. In his words, serious money, even with the split:

Wheel-man. A driver good enough to stop and block an armored car.

Safecracker for the strongbox inside.

Two heavy hitters to handle the guards and anyone else who got in the way.

And Vance, maker of plans and promises, all from the safety of his couch.

"We hit the truck," he'd said, being a tad liberal with "we." "Those security fuckos make twenty-five dollars an hour, they don't wanna die protecting money that ain't theirs. Hit 'em hard, Tyler. Hit 'em fast, and the five of us get paid."

Serious money. The kind that changed lives.

Or ended them.

❖

To Vance's credit, his intel was damn good.

Our wheel-man ended up being a wheel-woman—and Rosario drove a panel truck like a fuckin' Maserati. Boxed off the armored car in exactly the right alley, nice and tight. And when me and Sampson climbed out with AR-15 assault rifles and aimed them at the side windows, the guards just about shit bricks. That might have been more Sampson's doing than mine, though.

I'm substantial, sure, only a pound or two above my fighting weight of one hundred and ninety-five, but Vance's favorite attack dog was in a weight class all his own. Six-foot-six, pushing three hundred, and very few of those pounds were wasted. The guards practically fell over themselves giving us duffels stuffed with cash along with the huge strongbox, helpful almost. To the point where I was fairly convinced the goddamn box would be empty when we got it back to the country barn/safehouse and the Kid did his thing.

The Kid's name was Billy or Timmy or some shit, I couldn't remember—a twenty-something with a five-year-old's name—so everyone just called him "Kid," but lemme tell you, there was nothing childish about the way he could work a lock. He had that thing open in less than thirty minutes, and all of a sudden, the five of us stood around a table with half a million in cash and a velvet-lined case that the Kid had fished out of the bottom of the strongbox.

A case filled with diamonds.

Quarter-million on the low end?

Try three million, easy.

Unfortunately, that windfall pumped our armored car job up from serious money into ludicrous money, the kind that screwed the five-way-split math equation really quick. Betrayal is many things, primarily messy and dangerous, and in a room of proven criminals, all armed, serious money wasn't enough to make it look appealing—as far as my moral compass pointed, at least.

But three million? That created an entirely new world of possibilities, most of them shitty.

❖

We all come to a similar conclusion at roughly the same time, except for the clueless Kid, who pops a bottle of champagne he brought and starts pouring it into those cheap plastic flutes and passing them around. Vance, Sampson, Rosario, and I drink, staring at one another over the tops of our rims, while the Kid takes a mighty swig from the bottle.

Repeated swallows give each of us a few more seconds to think it over. Wonder who will draw first, whether there'll even be a conversation. One final opportunity to cut a new deal.

There isn't.

Vance lowers his champagne and turns to Sampson. Doesn't say a word, just nods.

Sampson's AR-15 is leaning against the table, and he grabs the stock and brings it to his shoulder, staring straight into my eyes. My own AR is across the barn next to the panel truck, so all I have is the 9mm Glock tucked in the waistband behind my back. I reach for it, already knowing I'm screwed, knowing I'll never get the gun clear before Sampson cuts me in half with a goddamn machine gun.

Before it happens to me, though, *Rosario* happens to Sampson. She rushes him from the side and plunges her only weapon—a switchblade—into the meat of his shoulder. The big man roars and inadvertently pulls the trigger on the AR, and it roars too, spitting bullets into the barn's roof instead of my spine.

If Rosario had been a little taller, or a little luckier, maybe managed to put the blade in his neck, she'd definitely have had a better chance of living. But she didn't, so she doesn't. Sampson drops the AR, wheels on Rosario and grabs her head with his gigantic paws. He twists until Rosario's neck pops, and like that, she's gone. I'm still fumbling with my Glock and the Kid just *stands* there, dumbstruck. Right up until Vance shoots him in the stomach. The Kid drops to my right and I move left, bringing the Glock up.

Vance has his little .38 revolver pointed my way now, and I *hear* his second bullet rip the air near my ear as I move. Without aiming, I lay down three quick shots in his general direction. One of them hits, and in the back of my mind I hear my father's voice after my first professional fight, when my opponent broke his own hand while punching my skull and had to forfeit: *Tyler, sometimes it's better to be lucky than good.* As Vance staggers, lowering his gun, I know Dad was right.

I stop running, aim, and put one in Vance's backstabbing heart.

I get roughly half-a-second of utter relief before realizing it's only Sampson and me now, and he's got an AR, which makes my Glock feel like a slingshot.

"You're DEAD, Buxson!" he screams. The AR goes off again, but I'm already running for the closest window. Diving through it. Losing the Glock in the process. Bullets splinter the wood behind me, and it's all the incentive I need to haul ass for the tree line. I'm on pure adrenaline, all reflex; no time to consider that everything on planet Earth that I need—the other AR, the truck, my phone, the money—is still in the barn. I only want to put some distance between me and the monster with a bazooka.

I hadn't given the surrounding farm area a moment's notice when we drove in, which is really unfortunate now, at sunset. The light getting worse by the minute... good for hiding, yes. But also bad for spotting danger headed my way.

I hide behind a thick oak and look back. Sampson is nowhere in sight. No noises come from within the barn. The Kid is probably still alive—he's gut-shot, but with a small-caliber bullet. As long as Vance's shot didn't sever an artery, he could hang on for hours. Long enough to survive, provided someone calls an ambulance. And provided some gigantic asshole doesn't finish him off first. For his sake, I hope the Kid can fake being dead until I figure out a way back inside the barn.

To my surprise, I *am* trying to figure a way back in. Not sprinting down the road, running for my life. That's losing the fight, no matter how long I live past today. My whole future is on that table, a new start, go legit, earn back some measure of respect. From my mom and dad, maybe even my brother.

Jessie.

The too-eager, hyper-annoying little boy that used to worship me. The loudest fan at every fight, win or lose. The hardest person to look in the eye after I'd sunk to petty theft to pay my bills.

Tyler, you were gonna be a champion, man. How could you do this?

The Kid reminds me of Jessie. Willy... that's his name, I think... and I'm pretty sure Willy deserves better than bleeding out on the dirt floor of a fucking barn.

So, I slip out from behind the tree and step into dying sunlight.

Trees, a tractor, and a strategically placed water trough provide enough cover for me to get to the front side of the barn. Huddled behind the trough, I peek at the deadly ground between me and the open barn doors: fifty feet that might as well be five hundred. With the sun setting behind the barn, the doorway is cloaked in shadow—and Sampson was smart enough to kill the lights inside. All I can see is an open maw, waiting for me.

Fifty feet. At full sprint, three seconds, maybe?

The panel truck is just inside the door, which means my rifle can be in my hands in less than five seconds. Unless Sampson is hunkered down inside the doorway, covering the open ground, I think I can make it. I take three quick breaths, peek one time before committing, and of course, see a muzzle flash from inside the barn. Bullets thunk into the sheet metal of the trough, and fetid water arcs through the holes to splash the dirt.

"Got you now!" Sampson yells, his voice getting closer. More bullets shred the trough, while I do my best to shrink. He's got me pinned down, nowhere to run, and unarmed, so he's walking forward as he shoots. Getting closer. Another fusillade of shots tears into metal, but then I hear the most glorious sound on God's green earth.

Click.

An AR's thirty-round magazine goes quick when you're rage shooting. If Sampson's got an extra, it'll take him at least a few seconds to clear the empty mag and reload a new one—and that's more time than it'll take for me to reach him. So, I scramble up from the dirt and go.

Right at him.

He's reaching for the new mag, head down, when I get there. All of my energy gets channeled into a flying kick, aimed square at his chest. Even three hundred pounds feels it when two hundred pounds rams it at full speed—Sampson topples over backward, while the AR and the new mag fly in opposite directions. The big man is down, but definitely not out, which means I've gotta get medieval, and fast.

I go after Sampson like I'm in the octagon again, desperate to maintain the advantage while my opponent is still disoriented. He flops over on his stomach and tries to push up, so I jump and deliver a power elbow to the back of his neck. Feels like I'm elbowing a side of beef, but the blow sinks him to the ground again. While he's down, I half-spin on top of him and ram my knee into the side of his face, as hard as I can. Twice. The second one results in a pleasing crunch.

I can do this. I'm gonna win.

Which is when he finally gets a massive hand on me. So goddamn strong. He pins me down and goes for my neck, to wrench my spine apart like he did Rosario's. I grab the hand at my throat, loop one of my legs over the top of Sampson's neck, and clamp the other leg around that one. A figure-four headlock... and I squeeze.

He's using his hand to choke me, which is bad. But I'm using my legs to choke him—and that's a race we both know I'm going to win. His free hand starts hitting my side and for a second, I'm thinking, *Is he really trying to tap out? He thinks I'll just let go if he asks?*

Then I see the blood and realize he's not tapping. He's stabbing. With Rosario's switchblade. I barely feel it with all the adrenaline, but it ain't a great development. I squeeze as hard as I can, Sampson's face transitions from red to purple, and the hand with the blade stops moving. Takes five more seconds for Sampson's steel neck muscles to slacken and his trachea to collapse.

I'm bleeding pretty badly by the time I find Willy. He'd crawled under the panel truck while Sampson went after me. There's bandages and gauze in the truck, and I do my best to patch us both up. It'll buy us some time, but we need more than a first-aid kit can offer if either of us is gonna survive.

"Tyler," Willy says weakly. I'm surprised the kid even knows my first name. "I can't believe you came back." He looks up at me with wide eyes and a dreamy smile. I've seen that look before. Misplaced hero worship, in all its glory.

"Yeah, well. Maybe there's a *little* honor amongst thieves."

Tears fill his eyes. "Thank you."

I grab my phone and dial 9-1-1, give them the address. After, I sit down next to Willy. "We'll see if you're still thanking me when we're both in prison. No way around that now."

"That's okay," Willy says, then coughs. He looks across the barn at Vance's and Rosario's corpses. "I'm beginning to think this career doesn't have a lot of long-term potential."

I laugh, and in spite of how much it hurts my body, my soul likes the laughter just fine.

Willy chuckles too.

"Maybe it's time for a fresh start," I tell him.

"That sounds nice."

So, the two of us wait for our fresh start on the dirt floor of an old barn, both content regardless of what form that new beginning will take.

Waiting.

Bleeding.

Hoping.

About the Author

Trey Dowell is an award-winning author of both short and novel-length fiction, specializing in crime, horror, sci-fi, and thriller. His short stories have been published in Ellery Queen Mystery Magazine, Abyss & Apex, MetaStellar, *and* Mystery Magazine, *among many others, and he won the 2022 Derringer Award for Best Crime/Mystery Short Story of the Year.*

An avid competition writer, Dowell has won many of the most challenging short fiction contests in the world, including NYC Midnight's Flash Fiction, Writing Battle, WritersWeekly.com, Bethlehem Writers Roundtable, and Bardsy's. His debut sci-fi thriller novel, The Protectors, *is published by Simon & Schuster.*

You can learn more at www.treydowell.com

ALMOST FORGET

BY MM SCHREIER

There's a faerie outside the front door. A tiny girl, no bigger than my thumb, just flying around the porch light with the bugs. Her gossamer dragonfly wings make a rainbowed contrast to the powdery whites and browns of the moths. I wonder if she had been on her way to some otherworldly ball when the light mesmerized her, for she wears a flowing gown woven of spider silk and moonbeams. A crown of dewdrops encircles her cornsilk hair. If she were human-sized, I'd be dazzled by her beauty—tongue-tied and blushing, despite knowing better.

Armored with an oven mitt and wielding a glass jar, I click off the kitchen light and ease open the front door. The dirty bulb over the porch emits a wan yellow glow, too weak to cast even a faint circle on the warped steps. I step softly, but the faerie pays me no mind as she circles the dim light.

I inch closer. A board creaks beneath my feet and I freeze, but the twilight creatures in the yard continue their nighttime activities. From the branches of a solitary oak beyond the house, a tree frog chirrups. A firefly blinks in the meadow, then another, and another. They flash their secret code in a syncopated rhythm. A gentle breeze rustles the tall grass where buttercups and daisies bob their heads in their sleep. It's the kind of perfect summer evening where I could almost forget there's a faerie hovering around the porch light.

Flapping wings draw my attention back to my mission. The fae girl elbows a brown flannel moth away from the bulb. While she's distracted, I leap up and capture her in the jar, my oven mitt clamping down to cover the top. The faerie shrieks and snaps at my hand. I pray the thick, quilted fabric will protect me from her needle-sharp fangs. Venom seeps through and my skin tingles.

I hip-check the door and stagger into the kitchen. The screen bangs behind me. Hopefully, the noise won't wake Opa. Snatching the jar's lid off the counter, I slap it on top and screw it down. The faerie rattles against the glass, but I ignore her as I shake off the oven mitt into the sink. My hand burns, palm turning red and blotchy. A rattled sigh escapes my lips as I inspect the skin—irritated, but unbroken. I flip on the tap and let the cool water ease the sting.

The faerie bares her fangs at me through the jar. I flick the glass with my nail. She hisses and pounds her wee fists against the side. Her wings vibrate in a multi-hued blur as her skin darkens to an ashy green. The ethereal beauty slips away, turned ugly by her trembling hatred.

Moonlight streams in the window and I close the blinds. Angry as a wasp, the creature continues to pummel the glass, but to me, her strikes are as quiet as caterpillar footsteps. Proud of my conquest, my imagined power, I grin and toss a dishtowel over the jar. Like a hooded hawk, she stills. She has no power in the darkness.

❖

In the morning, Opa wakes to find me drilling air holes in the jar's lid. He raises an eyebrow as he fills his coffee mug. Only the right brow. The left side of his face droops like melted candle wax—a memento of his own less fortunate run-in with faerie venom, many years ago.

Opa opens the fridge and sniffs the cream carton before pouring a dollop into his cup. He holds the carton out to me, silently offering, but I shake my head. He empties the last drops into his coffee and takes a deep swallow, never taking his attention off the jarred faerie. I can't tell if he's worried or proud. His eyes are silver-blue pools, deep and still, but I know there is a swift current below. Still, he speaks no judgment.

I put down the drill, and the little beastie removes her hands from her ears. Her lips turn downward and her wings sag. A tear trickles down her rosy cheek. If I were tender-hearted, I would be tempted to let her fly free, but one glance at Opa's scarred face is enough to silence such thoughts. I know better—her tears are the crocodile kind. I set the jar on the kitchen table with just enough force that she stumbles.

Onyx eyes glare at me, then her face splits into a sly grin. I realize my mistake. A golden beam of morning sunshine sifts through a gap in the blinds and illuminates the jar. Dust motes float like confetti in the light. They swirl toward the girl, drawn not by a breeze but by the fae's pull on the light-energy.

She raises her arms above her head and lets out a noiseless scream. As the sunlight pours into her, she swells, then drops her hands in a rush. At the same time, she stomps her bare foot. Power ripples outward in concentric circles like a stone thrown in a pond. A tiny crack spiderwebs the glass.

Opa leans against the chipped Formica countertop and takes another sip of his coffee. The tips of my ears burn in embarrassment as I dart to the window and secure the blinds. For good measure, I stand on a chair to tack up an old towel over them, careful not to let any more natural light slip in. A rookie mistake.

Two gazes follow me as I hop down, one angry, one measuring. My socks slide on the worn linoleum, and I grab the table to steady myself. Opa snorts into his bristly mustache. This is not going as I'd hoped. I rummage in a drawer and pull out a roll of tinfoil.

Crumple. Bend. Fold.

I create a metallic shroud for the jar. It will reflect the light and keep us safe from further fae antics.

Opa nods once. I take it as a sign of approval before snatching up my backpack. In my haste to catch the bus, I forget my lunchbox on the kitchen table.

❖

When I return home from school, Opa is fiddling with the jar. It appears he's tried feeding the faerie. Bits of my forgotten lunch litter the bottom of her prison—a scrap of peanut butter sandwich (crunchy, not creamy), a fragrant twist of orange peel, a teaspoon of congealing butterscotch pudding. She turns her nose up at it all.

Opa holds up a finger, and I pause. Curious, I follow him to the window in the living room where a fat housefly buzzes against the screen. This time, I'm the one with the raised eyebrow as Opa traps the insect in his cupped palm.

Together we return to the kitchen. I unscrew the lid of the jar, while he dumps the offering in. In a flash, I replace the lid. The fly bumps against the glass in an effort to escape, its wings humming faster and faster. Each thwack against the jar grows more desperate.

Like quicksilver, the faerie leaps up and plucks the fly out of the air. With one swipe, she rips its wings off and stuffs them in her mouth like potato chips. She swallows without chewing, and my stomach churns. Out of the corner of my eye, I can see Opa watching me, and I straighten my shoulders, choking back my revulsion lest I look weak.

The faerie chomps down on the fly's furry body and uses her fangs to tear it to gooey shreds. She grins at me, yellow-green liquid dripping down her chin. When she's finished, she uses one of the fly's segmented legs to pick bits of gore from her teeth. It's hard to believe I ever thought her beautiful.

Days march by and I continue to catch bugs to drop into the jar. At first, the faerie consumes them all in a vicious frenzy. Rip. Tear. Shred. It's not until a couple of weeks later that she grows less enthusiastic. At first, I think the gypsy moth I catch is not to her liking. Maybe she doesn't enjoy the baby-powder feel of its wings on her tongue. I go back to the houseflies, as they seem to be her favorite. A few more days pass and she loses her appetite for them as well.

The fight has gone out of her. She no longer rattles the glass and when she raises her head to bare her fangs at me, it feels halfhearted. Her hair is still cornsilk fine, but it's no longer golden, but autumn brown and drying. Coal-dark smudges ring her eyes.

I try leaving her out in the sun for a few minutes, peeling back the tinfoil barrier that reflects the light from the jar. She perks up, eyes brighter. Her wings flutter, catching the rays like a prism and scattering them into red-blue-violet splotches against the glass. I take care not to let her soak up enough energy to break the jar.

After, when I feed her a long-legged spider I find under the wood pile, she eats with more gusto, but her ferociousness is gone. She nibbles steadily and tidily. Opa chews on a toothpick as he watches. Quiet. Pensive. I know this look—so serious and thoughtful. There's a lesson he wants me to learn here, but I'm not sure what it is.

All I know is I've caged something vile, and with its captivity, the world is a little bit safer.

When I wake, there's an old woman lying at the bottom of my jar. Her hair is snowdrop white and her wings are translucent, as if they're carved of ice. Wrinkles crease her face and age spots dot the back of her tiny, gnarled hands.

I shake the jar, but she doesn't move.

After ripping back the tinfoil shield, I open the kitchen blinds. Sunlight floods the room, caressing the faerie's small body with its warmth. Not even a twitch. I peer closer. Her chest does not rise and fall with breath; her blank fish eyes look toward the sky.

Confusion wrinkles my brow, uncertain where I went wrong. I fed her and let her feel the sunlight on her skin. Faeries are supposed to be immortal.

Opa clears his throat. My eyes burn as I look up at him, but I blink hard to keep traitorous tears at bay. Why cry for a creature as nasty as a faerie? Still, my insides feel hollow and the anger I usually feel when looking at Opa's scars doesn't ease the emptiness in my chest. I set the jar on the table and slump in a chair.

A plank of wood clatters in front of me. I look up and Opa hands me his whittling knife, then wordlessly turns on his heel and leaves me alone. It's up to me to show him what I've learned.

I take up the knife and begin to carve.

Hours later, the sunlight through the window softens from gold to pink. I've finished. Folding the knife closed, I wipe the gritty sawdust from the table. My fingers feel stiff and a cramp twitches in my neck. I know now, it's a small price to pay.

I pick up my project and cradle the jar under my arm. Without being told, Opa waits for me under the old oak in the yard where he's dug a small hole, no bigger than the palm of my hand. Behind him, the sun slips over the horizon, painting the ground with lavender shadows. The scent of turned soil fills my nose, damp and loamy.

Kneeling, I open the jar and settle the faerie's body into her grave. I gently pat the earth around her as if tucking her in for a long nap. After smoothing the dirt, I prop the wooden grave marker against the base of the tree. The letters I carved on it are uneven, but legible:

All things deserve to be free.

Somewhere in the branches above, the tree frog warbles his song. It's both soulful and bittersweet. Twilight deepens from its soft lavender to velvet indigo, and the fireflies begin their blinking courtship dance. The summer breeze carries a hint of honeysuckle as it teases my hair into my eyes. Opa squeezes my shoulder.

It's the kind of perfect summer night where I could almost forget there's a faerie buried in the front yard. But I won't.

About the Author

MM Schreier is a classically trained vocalist who took up writing as therapy for a mid-life crisis. Her favorite stories are dark, emotional, and rich in sensory details. Much of her work uses a speculative lens to delve into the human condition and shine a light on things that make us uncomfortable.

MM is on the leadership team for a robotics company and tutors maths and science to at-risk youth.

Further works can be found in literary magazines and antholo- gies, as well as in two of her own short story collections. Monstros- ity, Humanity *explores the liminal space where the line between monsters and humans blurs, and* Bruised, Resilient *is a feminist collection showcasing how women experience the world.*

Follow MM Schreier online at www.mmschreier.com

THE HAPPINESS THIEF

BY ALEX TURNER-COHEN

"Money can't buy you happiness." But what if it could? What if happiness had a cost?

The year: 2048

Where other people saw suffering, Elliot Winston saw opportunity.

And the woman before him showed signs of immense opportunity. Jagged fingernails, clothes dangling loosely. She had glassy eyes, sad hollow pits inset into her skull. This lady looked like a prime victim—or should he say, customer.

"Good morning, ma'am," Elliot said, his gaze raking over her appreciatively. "What can I do for you?"

She stood in the office doorway, backlit by the flickering downstairs lights.

"Hi, um, I'm looking for Mr. Winston? The scientist?"

"Guilty as charged." Elliot plastered on his broadest smile, white teeth flashing like the opening of a shark's jaw. "I'm the owner of Borrowing Tomorrow's Happiness. Please, take a seat."

The woman sat on the edge of the leather armchair, as if to ensure a quick getaway. Borrowing Tomorrow's Happiness was situated above an adult-only store, so Elliot had tried to make up for location with style. Tiled floor, black leather seats. On his desk, a photo frame faced away from clients. A sign hung on the wall, swinging from its noose, reading: TRUE HAPPINESS IS ONLY A CREDIT CARD TRANSACTION AWAY.

And there was a safe at the far end of the office. The reason everyone came here—for the happiness vault.

"I'm looking to buy a day of happiness," the woman said.

"Then you've come to the right place." Elliot was a happiness dealer, though he preferred to think of himself as someone who made problems disappear—at least, in the short term. "Straight to business I see, Miss...?"

"Mrs. Daniels. Hope Daniels."

Her fingers were bare—he guessed she'd pawned off her wedding and engagement ring. *Perhaps her partner died in the suicide epidemic?*

"Pleasure to meet you, Hope."

They shook hands. He was circling his prey, and he liked his chances. He could smell her desperation like blood in the water—hot and enticing.

Hope scrutinized him. He imagined she quite liked what she saw. With dark hair and eyes to match, he considered himself rather dashing. Perhaps he was a little on the slim side but he wore an Armani suit which made up for it, with a button-up vest. The vest was an impulse buy; the seller said it made him look sophisticated, in control. Elliot couldn't help but agree.

"So, I just need a day of happiness. I've got the money." She spilt a wodge of cash onto the desk. They were tens and twenties whereas he needed hundred-dollar bills. How to put this delicately?

"Twenty-four hours of happiness, you say?" Elliot whistled, pretending that was a lot. "XD—eXtra Dopamine—is a very popular product, please understand. And I'm afraid you're just a little short."

"How many hours will this get me?"

Elliot sorted through the pitiful pile. "Twenty minutes."

"That's all?" Hope ran her fingers through her hair, leaving a greasy lock out of place. "He needs it... My husband needs a full day."

Clients rarely came here for someone other than themselves. A kind soul, then. Easier to exploit.

"Tell you what, I might be able to do something..." He let his sentence hang, like a dead man.

"What?"

"I could give you the happiness now, and you could owe me." Already she was shaking her head, but he held out a hand. "Hear me out. My business is a little—how should I say?—unorthodox." He licked his lips. "I have a Happiness Extraction Machine. You can pay me back in happiness at a later date. For the usual interest rate, of course. Twenty-five per cent. No need to worry about the money."

"You can extract happiness?"

He nodded.

"From anyone?"

"That's right."

"Then I have another proposition for you. What about you take a day of my happiness so I can give it to my husband?"

Elliot paused. "That's a most unusual request."

"So, can you help me out?"

"I don't see why not. After all, here at Borrowing Tomorrow's Happiness we pride ourselves on our customer service." Ever the businessman, he added: "For a modest service fee though. I'll keep a quarter of whatever you give. What do you say?"

Hope sucked in a breath. "Okay," she said. "We have a deal."

They shook hands. Elliot smothered a grin.

❖

"Just relax."

Hope lay on the black leather couch in the office. He rarely did happiness extractions here—usually his two heavies had to corner the client while he drained their XD.

As Elliot set up the Happiness Extraction Machine he was reminded of his days back in the lab, when he saw people as patients rather than potential profit. The machine targeted the anterior pituitary gland in a person's brain where the body stored dopamine. With tubes, needles, and vials sticking out of a little black box, it looked more like a torture instrument than the daily tool of a businessman.

"Will it hurt?" Hope asked.

Elliot's expression softened. He'd been scared for his first happiness extraction too, especially as he was the first human to ever try it.

"Not one bit," he lied. "Now hold still."

Inserting the needle into Hope's brainstem, he punctured the skin where the back of the head and the neck met. She gritted her teeth.

"Okay, I'm going to turn the machine on now." Elliot added: "Brace yourself."

Hope gasped. Elliot knew the feeling; it wasn't pain, not quite. It was the absence of pleasure. Hollow inside and out, a carcass picked clean, nothing but bones left.

The machine made an awful slurping sound as it extracted her happiness. Hypnotized, they watched the glowing liquid leave Hope's brain, snake down a tube and enter a little glass vial. Happiness in its purest, most usable form. He resisted the urge to grab some of the elixir and inject it straight into his body.

"Can I slip the XD into his drink or something?" Hope was saying. "If my husband knew I'd sold my happiness for his..."

"He'd feel too guilty to take it."

She nodded.

"Well, Mrs. Daniels, you're in luck. XD has no flavor whatsoever."

"It's our anniversary tomorrow," Hope said. "We've been married for five years. We're eating at the Crescent, that fish place. I've heard it's good. Expensive though. I just want him to be happy, even if it's just for a day."

Customers did this a lot. They thought because he was a happiness dealer, he was also a shoulder to lean on. Well, he might have figured out how to make happiness tangible, but that didn't mean he knew a thing about comforting people. That was someone else's department. Plus, he had his own problems.

"You don't need to explain yourself to me, Mrs. Daniels," he told her. "I've seen all sorts in here, believe me."

Blip. Blip. Blip. The extraction was complete.

"And you're done." He unplugged her from the machine, slapping a Band-Aid over the bleeding needle mark. "Here's your twenty-four hours, as agreed. The rest I keep. Pleasure doing business with you."

Hope couldn't even muster a smile as she took the proffered vials. She knuckled her eyes, as if this whole situation was a bad dream which would vanish once she woke up. No such luck, for either of them.

"Why do I feel... so empty?" she said at last.

"Because," he replied, "happiness has a cost."

◆

"Hope Daniels."

Elliot spoke her name aloud as soon as she left the office. He could still smell her perfume, the floral stink choking the air. There was something about her. Something that stirred old memories, buried deep, consigned to an underwater graveyard. Until now.

Hope reminded him... of *him*. Before everything. When he was Elliot Winston the scientist, who wanted to change the world, not Elliot Winston the entrepreneur. Before he'd lost Lilly. Before the mirror had shattered. Now he could only glimpse a distorted image of the man he'd once been.

Elliot glanced at the photograph on his desk. It had been a picture of him and his wife, Lilly. A tableau of happiness, the moment captured forever. Then lost. For two years he hadn't seen or spoken to Lilly. He wondered what she was doing now. *Does she ever think of me?*

Memories of Lilly had been too painful, so he'd replaced the picture with a pug. Not even his own pug—he was allergic to dogs. It was Doug the Pug, that funny-looking dog who was an internet sensation. The photograph ensured customers would think he had someone he cared for in his life.

Ironically, Elliot compared XD units with the feeling you get while watching a funny cat or dog video. Three funny clips equated to roughly five minutes of XD.

He placed the pug picture face down. There was a certain element of privacy needed for what he would do next. With trembling fingers, he opened the happiness vault. It was filled with vials, neatly arranged, containing XD. He'd been so excited when he first stumbled upon the happiness neurotransmitter. Oh, the possibilities! Although everyone was so connected with each other through technology, in real life most people felt more isolated than ever before. Maybe he could stop the epidemic, raise the World Happiness Index? Fix Lilly's depression?

Elliot unlaced his left shoe, threw it off, then rolled down the sock. His pale left foot glared up at him. He filled a clean needle with XD and, in one smooth movement, inserted the needle tip between his big and second toe. He squeezed. Dopamine flooded his body. Usually he felt like liquid fire was flowing through his veins but today he felt nothing. He grabbed a second vial, and a third until he felt a prickle of pleasure. Lying back, he closed his eyes, smiling.

◈

Elliot awoke in hospital. Lights glared, machines beeped. His gray skin contrasted with the white bedsheets.

"Ahh, you're awake," said the nearby nurse without looking up from her notes.

"What happened?" His cheek muscles ached as he spoke.

"Ambulance officers found you in a bad way. When they arrived you went into cardiac arrest. The defibrillator jolted your system back to life." Her eyes crinkled slightly in sympathy. A spoonful. No more. Measured out, just enough pity for each patient.

"Who rang the ambulance?" he asked, running his finger along his jaw. He remembered being in the office, alone. Then... nothing.

She glanced at her notepad. "An anonymous caller."

Last night he must have overdosed on happiness—he hadn't even known that was possible. That explained why his face hurt; he'd been grinning for hours. There was something absurdly grotesque about that image; he'd almost died smiling.

"What did you do to yourself last night?" the nurse asked.

He looked at her, puzzled. Then he looked around the rest of the room. Patients shuffled around the hospital with empty expressions. He recognized one of them. A former client. The man had bought a hundred hours of XD a few weeks back to help with his crippling depression.

With icy clarity, Elliot realized where he was—the psychiatric unit. He hoped no-one recognized him here as it wouldn't be good for business. A happiness dealer in a suicide ward? It was laughable.

"I recommend you get psychological help," the nurse was saying. "We have services available—"

"No need." Psychologists were capitalizing on the epidemic, charging upwards of a thousand dollars an hour.

"Is there anyone I can call?" the nurse was saying.

"No."

"Family, friends, partner?"

"No, there's no-one."

That made her look up from her notes. She paused for a moment and looked him directly in the eye. "Well, I'm really sorry, Mr. Winston, but we'll be needing the bed soon. Another suicide survivor."

"I'm not one of them, I didn't... I wouldn't..."

But as he left the hospital, he wondered whether his overdose had been an accident after all.

❖

Elliot's happiness vault was as empty as he felt. The door wide open, the metal shelves bare. Not a vial in sight. The hours, days, months of XD he'd hoarded—all gone. Disappointment hit him, a granite fist.

In his drug-addled state he must have left the vault unlocked and someone had taken it all. He didn't know whether to be angry or grateful. On the one hand, they'd stolen from him; on the other, they'd called an ambulance and saved his life.

His shoe crunched on shattered glass. Looking down, he realized the thief had dropped a vial. The glowing substance had spattered the floor like a blood stain. He went down on all fours and licked up some of the XD. A glimmer of glee shot through him, dulling the pain as his tongue bled from the glass. He saw a reflection of himself in the puddle. What a desperate soul he had become.

The happiness high only lasted a few moments. He needed more. His gaze snagged on something in the corner—a glass dome with a set of controls underneath. Thankfully, the thief hadn't realized its significance. It was a prototype of a new Happiness Extraction Machine. He'd pitched it to the investors as an XD magnet. Rather than attaching a needle to the subject's brain stem, the machine literally drained all the happiness nearby, without needing to make physical contact. He thought of his prototype as that annoying person at a party—the downer who sucked all the energy out of the room. Literally. Though he'd never seen if it actually worked.

It gave him an idea. If ever there was a time to test the thing, it was now. But where to go? More importantly, *who* to take from?

He knew just where to find the happiness he so desperately needed.

What he was about to do technically wasn't illegal, Elliot told himself. The idea was so new, the technology so evolutionary, that no-one had thought to criminalize it. He wasn't stealing, not really. He was just utilizing an untapped resource.

He reached The Crescent, a fashionable new restaurant, and there, in a prime seat by the window, sat Hope and her husband. Elliot ducked his head, but the couple were too busy floating in their own little bubble of bliss to notice him.

Elliot sniffed, nostrils flaring. Hope and her hubby were eating some kind of fish dish. When was the last time he'd shared a meal with someone? It was dinner for one at his place. Always for one. His eyes turned steely. If anyone had happiness to spare, it was the people in The Crescent.

Getting out the Happiness Magnet, he programmed it to *Maximum Drainage*. He set the timer to five minutes before detonation.

He studied Hope and her partner again. Hope wore heavy makeup, a huge amount of blush on her cheeks. Trying to put some color into her pale soul. She was smiling, but her eyes didn't crinkle at the corners. She was pretending to be happy for her husband. Just like Lilly had done with him, trying to spare him from her pain.

As for her husband, Mr. Daniels had too-bright eyes and a too-loud laugh. He fidgeted constantly—addicted already. Mr. Daniels' body subconsciously recognized that this wonder drug was coming from his wine glass; he sipped every few seconds and soon his glass was empty.

Hope refilled his glass and added more XD. The man would never know what this day of happiness had cost her. *But if he knew, would he thank her?* Elliot wondered. *Or would he feel something else? Anger? Disgust?*

Elliot's mind drifted to his own anniversary dinner with Lilly, two years ago. She'd been so happy that day—well, he *had* been dosing her drink, much like Hope was right now. He had treated Lilly to a fancy dinner and presented her with a beautiful silver necklace. Delighted, she asked how he could afford it on a lab researcher's salary.

And then he told her everything. How he'd wanted to stop the epidemic, come up with a cure for depression, so he'd isolated the happiness neurotransmitter in the human brain. He was now leaving his job at the lab to start his own business trading in happiness. Soon they'd be rich!

He'd expected her to be excited. She simply asked where the happiness came from. "From me at first," he admitted. "But now I get it from others. It's surprising how many people are willing to sell their happiness for a few extra bucks."

She said nothing. Her look said it all.

After the divorce, he began using XD. Now he couldn't stop.

Elliot looked at Hope and her husband again. They reminded him so much of himself and Lilly. It was an illusion of happiness that wouldn't last. That made him feel sadness. Or was it regret?

What have I done? In his desperation for XD nothing else had mattered. But now he saw the flaw in his plan—he didn't even know the outreach on his machine. As far as he knew, he could wipe out the whole city, stealing the happiness from everyone within a hundred-kilometer radius. All those people on the brink of suicide, clinging onto a thread of happiness, like Hope and her husband—they could be pushed over the edge.

He didn't want to cause anymore sadness. There was enough of that in the world already. More than enough.

Next thing he knew he was clicking buttons, trying to stop the magnet. Jabbing his fingers into the machine as if they were needles, he chose to *force quit*. Nothing happened. The machine was a prototype. It wasn't responding. He tried turning it off and on again. That usually worked. Again, nothing.

Four minutes until detonation. He opened the machine's hard drive then hesitated. It was essentially a bomb. If he pulled out the wrong wires, he would set it off ahead of time. In that moment, he realized he couldn't stop it.

Four minutes later, the XD magnet blasted. An invisible pulse shimmered across the city. People felt content for a moment. Then the feeling evaporated, as ephemeral as the happiness of watching a funny cat video.

Elliot had reversed the polarity of the magnet. Instead of taking everyone else's happiness, the drainer had taken his own. Then it had scattered his XD across the city.

Happiness has a cost, his own words echoed in his head.

There was not a single millisecond of XD left in his body. The machine hadn't just taken hours or days of his happiness—it had taken years. Everything he had.

And yet he felt... okay. His shoulders were lighter, the smile reached his eyes. A flicker of happiness coursed through his veins, from somewhere deeper, somewhere better. And for once, it had nothing to do with the drugs.

About the Author

Alex Turner-Cohen is an investigative reporter at Australia's national broadcaster. She has been a writer from a young age, winning her first award at twelve. She still hasn't recovered from the ending of Game of Thrones.

HIGHWIRE HEIST

BY MIGUEL A. RUEDA

The setting sun illuminated the New York City skyline in patches of early autumn dusk. A pair of black-clad figures stood on a roof's edge ten stories above 5th Avenue. They stayed in the shadows, out of sight from anyone who happened to peer up at the sky or out of the windows of the building they studied.

"Just playing devil's advocate here." Jackie stared across the bustling street while she twirled a toothpick between her teeth. "It can't be done."

"It can." A soft French accent flowed through Mateo's speech. "We've gone farther on bicycles."

"True, but as part of Les Acrobats Diminutive under the big top for Rowling Brothers Circus. That's in controlled conditions on a proper, *tested*, wire. There, it's easy-peasy, not an issue." Jackie pulled the toothpick from her mouth and used it to draw an imaginary line from their feet across the gap to the opposite rooftop. "However, from here to the other side of the street is a hundred feet, maybe hundred and a quarter. Normally a piece of cake, sure." She continued to use the pick to emphasize her points. "But here we've got to contend with cross winds and up-drafts, not to mention the flying rats and random trash blowing past."

"Risk versus reward," Mateo asserted, then continued. "It'll be our biggest score. By the time Cartier figures out what we stole, our troupe will be on the way to Philadelphia." He looked her in the eyes. "There's nobody better at walking the wire, and we've done outdoor work before. Remember the rain in Kansas? Even with a tornado warning, we performed perfectly."

She scoffed. "I remember Topeka, just not as fondly as you. What comes to mind is how that wind kept pushing us off the building while we rappelled from the twentieth floor of the Commerce Tower to break into that jewelry exchange seven floors below. Seemed easy on paper, but Mother Nature doesn't always play nice."

"Was a good payday though, wasn't it?"

"Sure, if you're curious about the price of potentially falling to your death, at least we have a benchmark."

Jackie popped the toothpick back into her mouth and started spinning it again. "You know, I grew up not far from here." She looked toward the sunset. "Over that way, a small town just across the Hudson; just my mom and me, although my aunt raised me. It's where I first studied gymnastics." She glanced uptown. "Mom and my aunt, her sister Francine, took me to the Met one year to see *Swan Lake*. I begged mom to let me take ballet lessons, but she said we couldn't afford it. Aunt Fran paid for them. She said to me, 'You have a desire in you that deserves to be satisfied.'" Jackie blinked hard, swallowed, and shook her head. "Old news."

"I've always wondered how you learned to be light on your feet, control your balance," Mateo said. "I've brought it up a couple times and you've avoided talking about your past. Why tell me now?"

Jackie walked while she spoke. "I guess I'm getting homesick, being this close. Haven't visited my mom's grave in years. I'm thinking it's time I give this life up, live a normal life."

"A dream." Mateo smiled. "You're a wanderer, not wired to settle down. We—" he touched her shoulder "—*you* can do this."

"Maybe I'm tired of the buses, the traveling. Everything smelling like it needs a wash even right out of the wash." Jackie turned back to the street. "You're probably right. We'll stick with the plan." She returned to using the toothpick as a pointer. "So, my guy with the city gave me the plans for the parade's banners that will be hung every four blocks up Fifth Ave." She nodded at a thick metal block attached to the building's parapet midway across the roof. "One goes here across to an identical block on Cartier's roof."

Mateo nodded as he gazed down to the avenue filled with people and traffic. "You're not concerned that people will see us?"

"Not really. Native New Yorkers don't look up. They're constantly scanning the sidewalk to keep from stepping in dog shit. Only tourists gawk at the tall buildings. And if any of those happen to see us, they'll just think we're part of the show that is 'The Big Apple.'" She waved jazz-hands to emphasize her point.

She continued, "My other guy at Cartier's said that they store all the loose gems in a safe in a hidden office on the top floor. It's only accessible through a secret door through a stall in the restroom. The owners never set the alarm on that door because it's inconvenient when they work late." She paced while she spoke. "There's only one night guard for the entire building. It takes him forty-five minutes to walk from the lobby to the top floor and he always starts at a quarter past the hour. Then he gets a fifteen-minute break to get back and start again."

Mateo smirked. "You know, it's hard for me to not feel as though I'm just *your guy* at the circus."

Jackie laughed. "The difference is that we share a bed, and I trust you with my life." She pulled him toward the roof stair. "Besides, you're the only guy I've got who puts the fun in funambulism."

❖

The faint stench of elephant dung, lightly sprinkled with popcorn, wafted through the arena. Spotlights snapped on to illuminate a lone figure resplendently adorned in a long green overcoat and bright red top hat, his dark skin a sharp contrast to his full white beard.

In one gold-gloved hand he held a microphone to his mouth. The commanding, resonant voice of Dakari Rowling, namesake and ringmaster of the circus, boomed through the speakers. "Ladies. Gentlemen. Tykes and tots of all ages. Above your heads is the pinnacle of high-wire, death-defying acrobatics. A mere human's most imaginative flights of fancy pale in comparison to what we have for you tonight." The crowd applauded in anticipation. "But first, we at Rowling Brothers Family Circus are obligated to afford those weak of heart the opportunity to enjoy the acts in our side rings." A spotlight followed Dakari's hand to his left. "Rolando The Conjurer. A prestidigitator of many talents. Prepare to be astounded by unexplainable acts of magic. Both large and small." A tall man wearing a shiny black tuxedo and bowler hat stood on a platform next to a table and a large box. He removed his hat and bowed.

Dakari swung his hand to the opposite ring. "And to my right, a literal dog-and-pony show presented by Boris and Natasha straight from the heart of Soviet Russia where they trained their animals to aid in their escape, in order to join us here in the greatest country on Earth, to perform just for you."

Another spotlight illuminated a couple wearing identical, tight-fitting, Russian military uniforms complete with dazzling ushanka hats. They stood in the center of the ring. Each held ropes attached to two horses. The horses pranced around the circle as though marching. On each of their backs, a small dog sat on a tiny saddle.

"For our main act." The spotlights followed Dakari's gaze upward. "Prepare to be amazed and enthralled by the gravity-defying escapades of Jacqueline and Mateo, Les Acrobats Diminutive!"

The audience turned their attention to the highwire far above their heads. Among the crowd, a single pair of eyes remained focused only on Jackie. Mateo stood in the center of the highwire, juggling bowling pins. Below him, a net hung mere feet off the floor.

Into his headset, imperceptible to the audience, Mateo spoke to Jackie. "Big crowd tonight. Very lively. We'll give them a good show, okay?"

"Always a good show," she replied through her own hidden mic. "They came to see the best." She paused and added with a chuckle, "And you too, I guess."

Jackie, now focused, said, "On my way." From a perch above Mateo's position, her knees wrapped around a trapeze, she swung upside down holding a bowling pin in one hand.

Mateo juggled and watched as she approached. At the last second, he launched one of his pins slightly higher, which allowed Jackie to catch it and release the one she had been holding back into the rotation.

Mateo never missed a beat. The crowd roared.

The pair, unique in their talents both in and outside of the big top, performed a mixture of tightrope walking, aerial acrobatics, and theatrics that no other duo dared.

During one of their more distinctive acts, Jackie walked onto the wire dressed as Marie Antoinette in an ornate ball gown and pouf wig. From the other end, Mateo approached as Louis XVI in full royal robes and perruque. Mid-span they exchanged wigs and clothing. The pinnacle of the routine happened when Mateo removed his flamboyant breeches by hopping straight up and pulling them off in one move, then Jackie would put them on using the same daring leap.

The crowd held their collective breath and exploded with relief when they completed the stunt.

Their act ended with their signature move. Into his mic, Mateo instructed their stage manager, "Drop the net." The large safety net lowered to the ground. This signaled the two floor acts to prepare their final tricks.

Mateo donned a blindfold and walked to the center of the wire. He said into his mic, "Go."

Jackie rolled out onto the wire on her back and stood, "First roll."

Mateo felt the wire vibrate and adjusted his center of gravity. "Go."

She rolled again. "Second."

Vibrate. Adjust. "Go."

"Third."

"Go."

Jackie now stood a yard from Mateo. "Final?"

"Final. Go."

On this command, magician Ronaldo knelt and lowered his head. From the other ring, one of the show dogs leapt off his horse's back, ran across the tent, and pulled off the magician's bowler, which magically released a dozen white doves trained to circle the big top just as Mateo and Jackie performed the spectacular climax of their act.

Mateo bent his knees and jumped straight up. The moment he left the wire, Jackie rolled underneath him and popped up on the other side.

At the apex of his jump, one of the doves flew too low and brushed Mateo's head, which caused him to flinch. The distraction broke his concentration and caused Mateo to miss his footing onto the wire.

"Falling."

Through instinct, Jackie spun, threw out her hand and snatched Mateo's forearm. When his weight pulled her off to the side, she flung out her legs and caught the cable behind her knees as she had held the trapeze at the start of their act.

Mateo's hand gripped Jackie's arm, slid down to her wrist, and locked their hands together. She said into her mic without a hint of urgency, "Got you." Both, strong from years of acrobatic work, held on.

Jackie instructed, "I'll swing away. On the return grab my other hand."

Without pause, he replied, "Go."

The crowd went silent. Some afraid that they might fall, most secretly hoping that they would.

Jackie rocked and Mateo grabbed her other hand.

She directed. "On three, spin and grab the rigging." The rough cable dug into the backs of her legs. She added, "And don't make it too pretty or we'll have to add it to the act."

On the third swing, Mateo released his hold, tucked under into a spin, and grabbed the cable with both hands.

The crowd jumped to their feet and applauded. Although many believed it was all part of the act, the other performers knew how close to disaster they had been.

❖

Jackie alternated bags of ice and hot water bottles behind her knees. "We got lucky, Mateo."

"Luck, it is said, is the result of opportunity presented with preparation."

"Who exactly said this? I'd like to meet them and give *them* a good thumping." She winced when she stretched her legs. "This job we're pulling, we need it for the future. We're not getting any younger, I almost dropped you. We should change the act, make it less dangerous."

Mateo smirked. "How long do you think Mister Rowling would employ us if we're not the daring duo who he advertises us to be? I am sorry about tonight, totally my fault. I lost focus when that dove hit me. I thought about what you said about pigeons, the... uh... flying rats, and—"

Jackie cut him off. "I forgive you. This time."

There was a knock on their dressing room door.

Mateo placed his hands together as if praying and bowed. "*Merci*. You rest your knees, I'll answer it. Probably Dakari wanting us to do that every night."

Mateo swung open the door to reveal a large, middle-aged woman dressed in a too-tight floral print dress covered with an oversized patchwork rabbit-fur coat. Her face unnaturally bronzed from extended sessions in a tanning bed, her curly hair overly poofed, her voice deep and graveled from decades of tobacco and alcohol. "You must be Mateo. Aren't you just the cutest little thing. I'd let you climb up one side of me and right down the other." She swept Mateo into a bear hug, his entire head engulfed in her bosom. "I'm Jacqueline's Aunt Francine; you can call me Fran." She gave him a wiggle and released him. "Where is that firecracker?" The scent of baby powder and *eau-de-something-cheap* clung to him.

"Aunt Fran?" Jackie grimaced when Fran gave her an identical hug to Mateo's, with the added bonus of lifting Jackie off the ground. Jackie squealed, "Ouch. Ow. I mean hello, what are you doing here?"

Fran looked around the room, studying every detail as though she'd be quizzed on it afterwards. "I saw you two tonight. That last trick really had me fooled. I thought for sure one of you was going to splatter right on the ground." She glanced at Mateo. "More you than her though; my Jacqueline is always in control." She began opening drawers and looking in their cases. "So, are you going to offer your favorite aunty a drink? You're only aunt, truth be told. I raised you better than to let a guest go thirsty."

"We have some wine?" Mateo offered.

Fran shrugged. "Any port in a storm." Then she winked at him. "And any sailor in a port, if you catch my drift."

Jackie exhaled. "Thank you, Mateo, wine will do." She offered a seat to Fran, then returned to icing her knees. "We legit almost lost it out there. It was Dakari's idea to include the other two acts in our finale. Always the entertainer."

Fran took a plastic cup of wine from Mateo. "Well, the whole thing was amazing. You made it look easy." She sipped. "Not easy really: well-practiced. You always had that way, making tricky situations look simple."

"Thank you, Aunt Fran, but why are you here?"

"Well, I saw the circus was in town and I wasn't going to wait for your invitation, so I bought my own ticket." She reached into her knock-off Michael Kors handbag and pulled out a receipt. "Cost a pretty penny and a prettier hundred-dollar bill, but well worth the investment." She held it out to Jackie. "I'll take cash. I'm sure you can get it reimbursed, like a retroactive comp."

Jackie grumbled, took the paper, and spoke. "Okay, I should have told you that I'd be in town. I was going to stop in on our day off to visit and then go to mom's grave."

Fran smiled. "I'm sure you were, darling, just like the last four times you were in town." She gave Mateo the side eye. "But I'm sure those unsolved jewelry heists the night after each of your last performances changed your plans. Having to skedaddle has that effect on some."

Mateo's eyes widened. Jackie rolled hers. "Aunt Fran, other than to be reimbursed—"

"Don't forget the cab and dinner. I have those receipts too." She started rooting through her purse. "Let's call it an even two-fifty."

"Other than that, why are you here?"

Fran looked up. "Dear, isn't it obvious? I want in. Who taught you how to scope out a job, pick a lock?" She batted her eyelids at Mateo. "Showed you how to use your feminine wiles to get what you need?" She looked back to Jackie. "Me." She downed the wine and held the cup out to Mateo. "Did she ever tell you about how when she was just twelve years old, she took some of my jewelry down to Peter's Pawn Shop all by her young self? Probably left out the part about Peter and me already having an arrangement and him calling me right up." She took the refilled cup. "I wasn't mad, mind you, just the opposite. This girl took that opportunity with no qualms about good or bad, or even hurting those who loved her. I took her under my wing that day. Never regretted it until she ran off to join the circus."

She spun to Jackie. "The circus, Jacqueline? Literally, the cliche of running away from home."

"I'm sorry, Aunt Fran," Jackie pleaded. "I needed out, needed a life away from that town. I got to see places I'd never have seen, pulled jobs we'd never have dreamed about until I met Mateo."

Fran chugged the cup and held it out again. "You really got nothing stronger? This cheap shit ain't going to make a dent in the itch I need filling."

Jackie laughed. "I'd forgotten what a way with words you have."

"I do enjoy a cunning linguist." Fran smiled at Mateo who desperately tried to look anywhere but at her. "Right, Mr. Mateo." Fran wiggled her cup. "It's crap, but it's all we got: keep it coming." He scurried over and refilled it. "So, what's your deal? Mateo, first name, last name, like Cher, only got the one?"

"N-no." He stuttered, visibly shaken. "Er, first name. I am Mateo Jacques Pelletier. I am *Québécois*."

"K-beck—who?"

"I am from Québec, in Canada."

Fran sat back. "Look at you Jackie, a foreign lover. Even if he is just Canadian, I've always wanted one of those."

Fran put her cup on a side table and leaned forward, placed her elbows on her knees, hands clasped in front of her. "Let's talk." Her gaudy rings reflected light in the room's lamps. "Those previous jobs, pretend another crew—one who just happens to possess your extremely specific talents—pulled them. Those stones weren't fenced anywhere on the east coast." She looked back and forth between the two to make sure they were paying attention, even though there was little chance they weren't. "Peter, you remember, with the pawn shop, he's retired, but his son, Pete Junior, took over and he's expanded up and down the coast, so he'd have heard something about them being moved. But he hasn't, and that upsets him." She sat up. "Upset me too if that mysterious crew had a connection to me and didn't offer an opportunity at a taste. Just a lick." She shot a glance at Mateo who quickly looked down at his feet. "What I'm saying is that Junior remembers you and asks about you. You did go to prom with that boy, didn't you? He still gets googly eyes when he talks about you. I'd swear he must have gotten his cherry popped that night to hear him go on about it. But that's your way, isn't it. Get others to give you what you want and then move on."

Fran slapped her knees and stood. "Well, I'm off to meet with your ringleader, I mean, master." She looked at Jackie. "We all know who the actual ringleader is, don't we?"

Fran took a small handkerchief from her coat pocket. "I met Dakari on the way in, introduced myself, and he invited me back to his room for a nightcap." She closed her eyes. "That dark chocolate Adonis has such big hands."

Without mentioning why, she used the cloth to wipe down the cup she'd been using and placed it back on the table.

She asked Mateo, "You know what they say about men with big hands, don't you?"

Mateo shrugged. "I... no. What do they say?"

"They wear big gloves." She laughed.

Mateo chuckled nervously and sipped his wine.

Fran licked her lips. "And by gloves, I mean condoms."

Mateo's cheeks bulged as he choked back his wine.

Fran's laugh was reminiscent of a witch boiling a toddler for her breakfast. "Oh my, Jacqueline, your boyfriend is just too easy."

Without thinking, Jackie blurted out, "He's not my boyfriend."

Mateo's eyes darted to her. "*Qu'est-ce que?*"

"Oh." Fran covered her mouth. "You didn't know. You thought..." She glared at Jackie and walked to the door. "Men's hearts are just another jewel for you to steal, aren't they?"

She used the handkerchief to open the door.

"Well, I'll leave you to it. Consider my offer. I really do miss you. Junior misses you, and you could probably—who am I kidding—could *definitely* work him for a few extra points. You can pay me back for the ticket at home." She leaned in and whispered, "And don't worry, kids, I won't tell Dakari any family secrets, but I may unearth a few hidden treasures." She winked at Mateo and left.

Mateo sat in silence, twirled his cup, and studied the wine's surface. "If anything were to ever happen to you, I would be lost. You're the only one who understands what it was like for me growing up."

Jackie sat beside him. "I'm sorry, Mateo. I thought you understood: we're just friends who work together and, considering what we do on the side, that's no way to have a real relationship. We're vastly different people. I was raised by a weird aunt in the suburbs, and you grew up in a pristine Canadian countryside in your family's circus."

Frowning, he said, "They made me work since the day I could stand. I only stole from them so I could move to America and make my own act. For love of the work, for myself. This Cartier job is for us. For our future."

"Mateo, I know it was rough, but you chose to leave." She lifted his chin to look into his eyes. "You grew up in a world of the circus learning all the tricks of that trade, while I was growing up in the world of the street, learning all the tricks of our other trade. The one that makes us real money. Together. It's why we're such an effective team."

He glared. "Just a team to you, not to me." He pulled away. "We can take the money and move to where I came from. It is beautiful there. Peaceful."

Jackie shook her head. "When did either of us want peaceful? We risk our lives and freedom every day." She threw up her hands. "Besides, I can't get a passport, you know that. Not with my record."

"I want to go home," Mateo said.

"What do you mean? The circus is your home."

"Mont Tremblant."

"What?"

"It is in Canada."

"I know where it is. I thought you couldn't go back. What exactly are you saying?"

"My sister sent me a letter. My mother is ill, and she asked for me to come back. She said that all is forgiven. The money, me leaving, she says they understand, and I want you to come with me."

She stood, grimacing. "How about we talk about the future when we have enough money to get us there."

She limped over to her large traveling trunk, opened a hidden cover, and removed blueprints and a set of drawings. "The city will be quiet the day before the parade. And with the store closed for the celebration, they won't notice anything missing for a couple of days."

Laying the papers on a table, she said, "These are the floorplans to Cartier's and a mechanical drawing of how the banners are attached across the street. Let's plan our short term out first. No point in counting our chickens, or diamonds in this case, before they hatch."

❖

In the darkness on the rooftop, the distance across, and the drop to the street, seemed more treacherous than in the daylight when they had scoped out the job.

Mateo stood by the parapet—the thigh-high wall that ringed the roof—and looked down. "Not too late to call this off," he said. "I know your knees haven't healed; I noticed during today's performance."

Jackie flexed her legs. "I'll be alright."

"It is not you I worry about," Mateo snapped. "We both need to get across to do this job. We are a team, no? Or is that only the case when you need me? Your *guy* in the circus."

Taken aback by her partner's shortness, Jackie replied, "Whoa, we're still hung up on this? And don't you mean we need to get across *and back*? I don't plan to hang around to watch the parade from over there while we wait for the cops to arrive."

Mateo softened. "Of course, sorry. Just butterflies. This rope they use for the banner is bigger than what I'm used to." He put his hand out over the edge and bounced the line. "And it's too loose."

Jackie grabbed a large yellow lever at the attachment point of the cable to the roof. "This adjusts the tension. Watch." She stepped on a red pedal on the side of the mechanism. "You have to keep pressure on the release pedal while you pump it." Jackie lifted and pumped down twice; the cable stiffened. She lifted her foot off the pedal. "Just don't lift your foot while the lever is up, or the cable will play out."

Mateo relaxed. "I will use all those tiny butterfly wings to help us float across." He hugged Jackie, adjusted his earpiece, and pulled a black balaclava over his head. "We are a team."

She kissed his head, then pulled on her own mask. "Go."

Stepping up onto the parapet, instincts took over.

Mateo looked straight across at his destination, never glanced down or to the side. The feel of the cable beneath his feet comforted him. Halfway across, he felt the cable vibrate as Jackie stepped out.

Ten stories below, six New York natives studied their phones, while a full MTA bus, three taxis, and an NYPD cruiser passed without noticing the pair as they walked across the parade banner.

The only witnesses to their nocturnal act were a pair of Italian tourists who applauded when they reached the other side.

Mateo stepped onto Cartier's roof and headed for the skylight, knowing that Jackie would be behind him. He used an electric screwdriver from his backpack to remove metal screws from the window frame. The metallic grinding of the motor amplified every time it slipped and threatened to strip the head and end their night before they were able to get inside.

Jackie tied a pair of climbing ropes around a thick chimney and checked her watch. "The guard has already started his round. We have forty minutes left to do the job and get the skylight back in place."

Mateo removed the glass, Jackie dropped the ropes, and they climbed down.

They entered through the secret bathroom entrance and found the safe behind the desk. It took fifteen minutes for Jackie to crack it. They emptied the contents into Mateo's backpack and headed back to the ropes.

All had gone exactly as planned; neither had to utter a word inside the store.

When they climbed back onto the roof, the night air was still as hot and humid as it had been when they'd walked across the banner. The scent of a brewing summer thunderstorm in the wind carried the promise of rain as faraway thunder echoed off the buildings. Sharp gusts buffeted them.

Mateo had begun to install the window frame when Jackie pulled him back. She pointed through the window. "He's early." The sharp beam of a flashlight played against the walls below them and focused on the floor beneath the windows.

Mateo peered through the grimy glass and saw the light focus on flecks of dirt and paint which had been dislodged when they had climbed inside.

Mateo jumped back when the beam swung upwards. They heard the sharp clap of the guard's shoes against the polished floor as he ran from the hallway.

"Run," Mateo shouted.

Jackie stepped up onto the parapet. "The wind is pulling the banner like a sail. We'll have to go one at a time."

He held out the backpack. "You go first. If the guard comes up, I'll slow him down."

"But..."

"I'll be right behind you."

She took the pack, lifted her mask and pulled Mateo's above his lips. She kissed him. "I'll never forget you."

Jackie held out her arms to help with her balance as she cautiously walked across. A strong gust buffeted the banner. She felt the line of the rope through her thin-soled shoes—in her mind she imagined each foot as that of a monkey's paw gripping the rope as she moved forward.

Riding the undulating line as a surfer would a wave, she was one with the unpredictable chaos of the wind and rope. She jumped off the parapet and turned back and saw that Mateo had already climbed up on the other side.

When he fixed his gaze across the gap, she stepped onto the red pedal, held up her hand, and whispered into her mic. "Wait."

Through her earpiece she heard him. "Why?"

Without breaking eye contact, she pulled up on the lever. "I'm sorry."

She lifted her foot. The line wound out and draped the banner across 5th Avenue.

Behind Mateo, Jackie watched the stairway door open; the silhouette of a man holding a gun emerged. Over the wind and the slap of the loose banner, she heard Mateo. "Jaqueline?"

"I'm not looking for a home. Or peace." She held up the backpack. "I have the goods; you're not holding anything hot. At worst, they'll charge you as an accomplice and they'll deport you. You'll be able to go back to your family and have both. Home, and peace."

Jackie heard Mateo say the last thing he'd ever say to her.

"Go."

About the Author

Miguel A. Rueda was born in Manhattan NYC. His short stories have been published in several anthology collections in various genres including horror, science fiction, historical fiction, and one which he will readily admit that he's surprisingly good at, romantic comedy.

He lives in northern New Jersey with his wife and their pack of unruly dachshunds and a kitchen cat.

In his spare time, he tinkers with a classic car which is barely younger than himself and has been an avid motorcyclist for over five decades.

Miguel writes under his given name and his pen name, Wayne Hills.

The Cherry-Pie Files

by Trond E. Hildahl

"You cut us out again, you get cut."

Paul reminded me of the villain from the cheap late-morning feature. All swagger, no brains. But he ran book for the local outfit, so he had plenty of smarts as well as a big stick backing up his big words.

"It was one weekend playing the ponies with 'Happy' Jones instead of you." I sighed. "Besides, I hit the trifecta of Loser, Nag, and Dogfood. I'm broke—I won't be a betting man for a long time."

"Okay, Richard, you squared up your tab last month. You get that far behind again, though, and I'm calling Frankie." He paused at the doorway to my inner office. "I have a feeling you like your kneecaps, right?" I gave him the old-fashioned salute as his back turned. As I stalked back to my desk, I could hear the bell on the outside door jangle.

"Good riddance, you rat." Rummaging around in the lower drawer, I found what I needed. But the day took an even lower turn: the bottle of scotch was empty. Just like my bank account. Just like my client list.

The white clapboard sign outside read, "Richard Lipsky, Private Investigator. No Job Too Small, Rates Negotiable." But lately, even the minuscule jobs seemed out of reach. Not so much as a reward for a lost dog had come my way.

I checked myself before throwing the bottle against the wall. When they tossed me out of this miserable hole, I was going to need my security deposit back. Contenting myself with a kick at the desk, I collapsed in my chair to check my cell for messages.

"Is this a bad time?" I heard from the doorway.

I looked up. So did my day. The dame standing there was butter, over cream, over a single malt scotch. There were dangerous curves sliding directly to heaven, topped with long raven hair spreading around... a very sad face with puffy eyes.

"I came in just as that man was leaving," she said. "You are Richard Lipsky, right? I could come back?"

"Yes, no," I replied. I shot to my feet and went to greet her. "Come in, what can I help you with?" I handed her to the guest chair and perched on the edge of my desk, blocking her view of the empty bottle.

She sank into the easy chair like summer rain: warm, dark, and leaking tears. "It's my boyfriend, Jimmy Marshall. My former boyfriend, I should say."

Damn women and their crying. I'm a sucker for the old damsel-in-distress act. "Why 'former'?"

Sobbing harder, she managed, "Because he's dead!"

❖

Tissues and my charming disposition soon had her composed.

"Okay, Miss...?"

"I'm Margot. Margot Robinson." She managed a smile and the room brightened visibly. "Jimmy was an accountant for the Smithers Meat Packing Company. He called me late last night to say that he'd found something badly wrong at work. When I asked what it was, he said he didn't want to involve me; that he needed to get out of town quickly, that it was..." Her voice caught and I thought she was going to turn the waterworks back on, but she was tougher than she looked. "That it was over. He sounded scared. Then he hung up on me!"

"So what did you do?"

"I drove to his house. When I got there, we had a terrible row. Then we smelled smoke, so we got out. Flames started shooting through the roof. Jimmy was frantic. He yelled something about proof and cherry pie and ran back inside."

I jotted down Jimmy's address on my trusty yellow pad, legal size. Then *cherry pie = proof?* and underlined it.

She gulped. "That's the last I saw him. The fire department came." Margot closed her eyes. "They brought Jimmy out in a bag."

"I'm so sorry, Miss Robinson." I took her hands in mine. "I need you to think back. Was there anything strange or different when you got there?"

One hoop earring swayed as she cocked her head, considering. "I had to park around the block from his house. I walked by a man connecting something to the back of a large truck." She opened her eyes. "It was a dark color, I couldn't really see it even in the streetlight. It had oversized mud flaps?"

"What about the man?" I pressed.

"I don't think I'd seen him before. He was short, maybe? It was dark, and I just wanted to get to—get to—"

And the dame broke down again. I was going to have to order more Kleenex.

I did a web search on Smithers Meat Packing Company while she dabbed at her eyes.

Facts: local, second-generation business. Owned by Amanda Smithers-Whiting. Fifty-two, married to Carleton Whiting, no children. Carleton managed the packing plant, which was worth a cool ten million.

Opinion articles, page-two links: Carleton Whiting had big plans for the company. He had overactive glands, several girlfriends, and most importantly, an ironclad pre-nup. And he was connected, via rumor and whisper, to Frankie Moreno.

Yeah, the same Frankie whose underling was so concerned with the health of my kneecaps.

"So, Miss Robinson, what exactly do you want me to do?"

"Call me Margot, please. I think Jimmy discovered that the company was doing something illegal, and Mr. Whiting had him killed. I... I want you to find the truth about what happened to Jimmy!"

Smithers and Whiting was the largest game I'd gone after, but I didn't feel like mentioning it. Besides, every time I wrote a check lately, I dropped it first to see if it would bounce.

"Miss Margot, I'm a hundred an hour plus expenses, with a grand up front. But I'll find out if your Jimmy died a natural death or not."

She chewed her lip. "I'm not minting money. How about four hundred in advance, seventy an hour, and I'll be your gofer on the case?"

I'd had to try.

"Deal. Let's split up—I'm going to the scene of the fire and then the Coroner. Why don't you bull in on the Smithers facility and see if you can find out anything from the employees? We'll meet back here at three."

"Thank you, Mr. Lipsky. I'm on it." She paused. "Oh! Since you're going there, Jimmy always joked about having a safe in the kitchen? I never saw it, though."

She left. I hummed while straightening up the office. Even a few billable hours before concluding that the fire was just an accident would help my accounts payable. But the bell announced Margot's return within seconds.

"Yes?" I stuck my head into the foyer.

It wasn't the dame. It was Frankie Moreno. Nattily dressed in a custom dark-blue suit, he had his trademark bowler hat in hand as he stepped inside. He proffered his hand.

"Ritchie! I shoulda had a longer conversation with Paul before he came knocking. You, my friend, are a special case. You walk our line and you have to tiptoe the blues too. No hard feelings?"

I couldn't afford mac and cheese, I *really* couldn't afford to be on Frankie's bad side. He was the capo. He knew everybody. And he had Big Vinnie, standing watch outside the door.

"No hard feelings. And hey, I might take a couple ponies this weekend after all."

"New job, eh? Is it that doll that just walked out? Man, she's fine."

"Yeah. As long as the purse is full, I'm her man."

"I've been single for too long, Lipsky. She's a ten." He smiled, all the gold on his teeth glittering. "Maybe I could be her man."

"She is recently single."

"There you go! Hey, can I help you out, here? Get on her good side?"

I blinked. Dapper Frankie playing gumshoe? Laughable.

"I truly hate to say no to you, Frankie, but this one is business before pleasure."

"Okay, Ritchie, you're the boss." He rolled his eyes. "Here. But I'm gonna be around. Your lady friend is a keeper."

❖

Sixty-Eight Elm Street was in a nice neighborhood. It was the kind of place where old men yelled at kids playing stick-ball in the streets and everybody came running when the ice-cream truck made the rounds.

The front of the house still looked intact but the back and roof were charred and ruined. Leftover water pooled in the ruts left by the fire trucks. I saw crime tape spooled around the entrance but no lookie-loos, so I ducked under the yellow line and used the key that Margot had passed me.

The carpet in the hallway squished under my boots. Without power in the house, I used my cell phone flashlight app to find my way. Where? Jimmy had had some fetish for cherry pie. You make that in the kitchen—plus an invisible safe?—so I figured that was a good place to start.

The room had large windows, now broken open, letting in plenty of light. Shattered glass crunching under my feet, I spun in a circle from the center of the room, taking it all in.

No safe, unless it was more cleverly hidden than anything I'd ever heard of. *So, we do this the old-fashioned way.* The freezer was always the first place I checked. Then the shelf above the freezer. Nobody ever looks up. Next came the odds-and-ends drawer; people think their stuff is protected if mixed in with batteries, thumb tacks, and old keys they can't remember opens what.

Zilch.

I rummaged through the cupboards. No dice. Shelves? Just dishes, baking-ware, cookie sheets. I straightened up, back hurting.

Cherry pie. I bent once again, on a hunch.

The baking stuff included stacked pie tins emblazoned with a blood-red cherry. Upon inspection, tin numbers two and three were stuck together in an odd fashion. Something rattled: after I pried them apart, a USB flash drive clattered onto the floor.

That was my meal ticket. I might have to order some cherry pie at Flo's Diner in celebration tonight. It was time to scram.

I'd just closed my car door when a black-and-white cruised down Elm. It stopped right outside the late Jimmy's home, so I shut off the ignition to watch the show.

The two officers were inside for half an hour. When they exited, I was standing against a telephone pole, smoking a cigarette. I know: those things will kill you.

They wasted no time with pleasantries.

"Well, Lieutenant Johnson, if it ain't Private Investigator Lipsky in the flesh."

"I see him, Detective Ramirez. I sure am puzzled why an ordinary guy is loitering around the scene of a death and fire."

It was time to stop their patter. "Detective, Lieutenant. Find anything interesting in there?"

Ramirez laughed. "This here is *oh-fish-shell* police business. We're just doing our job and asking you to move along like a good little private citizen."

I stood my ground. "Cause of fire?"

Johnson relented. He would usually chat if Ramirez didn't put his foot down. "Fire chief said there was an accelerant at the back of the house, probably gasoline. Funny thing is, that makes two last night."

"Really?"

He scowled. "And a death in that one too. Amanda Smithers—the lady that owns the meat-packing plant. Homicide is busy today, so just let us do our job, okay?"

"One more question?"

"You're a pain in the ass, Lipsky."

I was dancing with both shoes off, but my gut said to push him. "Off the record, I have a confidential informant who saw a limo here last night. Any limos seen at the other fire?"

Johnson shook his head. "Some big truck, huge mud flaps. No limo—"

Ramirez elbowed him. "That's enough. Say, Lipsky, why don't you button your lipskies and get the hell out of our case."

This is as interesting as a peephole, I thought. Margot remembered a big truck as well. Same vehicle, two fires, two deaths. It was time to see Dr. Chaudhary, the coroner. And I was itching to see what was contained in that flash drive—some cherry-pie files, so to speak.

❖

I had a nice little understanding with the doc. He never kept me waiting. He didn't worry about patient confidentiality, at least not post-mortem. He enjoyed handing me a manila envelope with a few Benjamins and a list of horses' names. And he loved getting a much thicker envelope back, albeit less frequently.

"Doc, tell me about Amanda Smithers-Whiting and Jimmy Marshall?"

His hands shook as he lifted his coffee cup. "I don't know if I can assist you, Richard."

"Just the basics? Help me out."

His eyes flicked to the door. Making sure it was secure, he whispered, "Mrs. Smithers was DOA, third-degree burns. We needed dental records to positively ID her. The male died from a gunshot wound."

I was worried my eyebrows would climb all the way off my face. "GSW? I thought he died in a fire too!"

His voice grew formal. "I apologize, Mr. Lipsky. I am so very busy today. I must ask you to leave."

But he still handed me an envelope.

❖

As I unlocked my office door, I heard a klaxon go off behind me. Frankie, eyes like little beady jewels, was staring at me from the passenger window of the largest, greenest, pickup truck I'd ever seen in my life. Vinnie let off the horn.

"Yo, Ritchie."

"Nice wheels, Frankie."

"Thank you." The velvet left his voice. "This girl, Ritchie. Your new client. She's got you looking at this Jimmy guy's death. What's he to her?"

"Boyfriend. Or, was."

"Gal's gotta have closure, right? Maybe she'll be on the rebound."

It terrified me how his voice could flip from edgy to friendly in the span of a heartbeat.

"My friend, I think I need to offer you some advice. Will you take it?"

"I always listen to my friends, Frankie."

"I think you ought to know that she is not only a beautiful woman, but she is a dangerous woman as well. She's packing, concealed weapon permit. Did you know that?"

"News to me."

"Personally, I admire beautiful, dangerous creatures. I will see you later, and maybe her too. Good day, Ritchie." The window slid up. As the truck pulled out, I couldn't help but notice the most enormous mud flaps on the back of that monstrous truck.

Bemused, I tried a second time to unlock my door. And was interrupted by another car horn.

I turned again, saw Margot's car pulling up. I walked around to open her door, wrinkled my nose.

"Phew. Your car is a bit..."

"Stinky? Yes, I think I have a leak in the exhaust."

"Smells more like straight-up gasoline. You might want to have your tank checked." I stopped short, remembering *two* cases of accelerant fires. "Unless you keep a few gallons in the trunk for an emergency?"

She either had no clue what I was insinuating or had a better poker face than the guys in my Friday-night group.

"Thanks, I'll have my mechanic check that out."

Inside, she lit up with a manic grin. "I visited the Smithers plant. They were real talkative, especially Carleton. And you won't believe what happened."

I positioned my notepad. "Go."

"Mrs. Smithers-Whiting died in a house fire last night too! Can you believe that?"

"You don't say?"

She deflated with my lack of reaction. "It sounds like Mr. Whiting stands to inherit the whole fortune, with no other heirs on the Smithers side. He expressed his condolences at Jimmy's death. He promised he'd make it right and make sure I was taken care of even though Jimmy and I weren't married. He seemed real shaken up when I said I was Jimmy's pregnant girlfriend."

That was a sucker punch. "You didn't happen to mention that this morning."

"I'm not really." She flashed an impudent smile. "But I'm a PI, now, Mr. Lipsky. It seemed the right thing to say, to prompt a reaction."

I could only nod my head in respect. She was a quick study. This might be a good time to spin the chair in the other direction.

"Quick question: do you own a handgun, Margot?"

Her poker face was still in play.

"Sure do. Sorry, was I supposed to tell you?"

"It's no biggie." I dropped my pen to the desk and sat back.

"Oh! One more thing. Carleton's secretary took a call while I was waiting. He's having dinner tonight at a famous Italian restaurant with some VIP named Francis."

"I'll add it to my notes. Okay, Margot. I have some research to do. Go home and get some rest, kid." I looked again into her green eyes. "Margot?"

"Yes, Mr. Lipsky?"

"Call me Richard, please. Margot, you might wanna make sure you have your piece close around you."

When she left, I opened Dr. Chaudhary's pony rides. The contents were surprising: there was a surprising lack of green bills, but instead, two official-looking forms. One was the original death certificate for Jimmy Marshall. It showed COD as asphyxiation/smoke inhalation. The second was a duplicate—but time-stamped three hours later. I stiffened, hairs standing out on my neck. COD on that one was three letters: GSW. Gunshot wound.

I slid the flash drive into my PC. Reading until my head throbbed, the afternoon flew by.

◆

If there was a formal occasion in the city at a "fancy Italian trattoria," they were talking about Regatazzis. But I had time. I made a couple of calls from the office and then I went home.

On a normal night I'd curl up on the couch with the remote and a bottle, hoping dawn would arrive before the headache. Tonight, though, I showered, shaved, and took so much care with my hair it would impress Vinnie-the-Muscle.

I picked Margot up at seven, as agreed on my first call. She was stunning. A dark-green dress sheathed her slim form, while her black tresses were piled high in an intricate weave. Cosmetics covered the damage the day's grief had caused.

I whistled. She smiled.

Dusk had arrived, and the valet sneered at my little Civic. I checked my pocket for the USB drive before he drove off.

Lights were strung up across the entry and fat wine bottles stuffed with candles hung from the ceiling. A band was playing from farther inside, but I only had eyes for Lieutenant Johnson.

"You called, Lipsky, I came. You better have something good. Otherwise I'm driving you to a different destination than you had in mind. And the food ain't as good there as they serve at this joint."

"You're going to thank me, Lieutenant. Here." I presented the flash drive.

He took it dubiously. "Tell me."

"This drive contains accounts from Smithers Meat Packing Company. They have several transactions that deserve your attention. Many are checks drawn on the company's accounts to pay for Carleton Whiting's girlfriends."

"That's not really my area, Lipsky. Sounds like the IRS might want to eyeball it, but not me."

"You might change your mind, Lieutenant. Jimmy Marshall, the late accountant at Smithers, copied these files. He also noted on them that he confronted Whiting last week, saying he would not hide the transactions anymore or sign off on them for the annual reports. Jimmy, coincidentally, was the man who died at the Elm Street fire last night."

Johnson sneered. "But he died from a bullet. In fact, your lady friend there is now a person of interest in that case. We received an anonymous tip that her handgun is the same caliber that shot Jimmy."

Margot gasped.

"Not so fast, Lieutenant." I handed him a folded packet. "This is the original COD showing Jimmy died of smoke inhalation in the fire. The certificate was later tampered with to show GSW."

Johnson glowered.

"Back to the account transactions," I continued. "More checks are made out to a Francis Moreno and his bookie Paul Canta. Several are for bets on horse races, but the last two transactions from Carleton to Francis are the most intriguing. Two days ago, there were two separate hundred-G payments. And last night, Francis used his new oversize toy truck to drive to two homes. He set two fires. He killed two people."

Johnson's face tightened. "You couldn't have come to the office with this? I have to put out an APB on these bastards."

"Why do you think I asked to meet you here? My partner here—" Margot beamed like a lighthouse saving a ship from the reef "—found out that Carleton Whiting and Francis 'Frankie' Moreno are both here tonight for dinner."

Johnson got busy on his radio, a gleam in his eye. He looked up after a few exchanges.

"Lipsky, I'm impressed. Maybe I'll buy you guys dinner at Flo's sometime."

I shared a smug grin with Margot.

"Flo serves a mean cherry pie."

About the Author

Trond E. Hildahl lives in Southern California. An IT professional by day, night (plus caffeine) transforms him into a creative.

His work has been published on SciFiShorts *and in several anthologies, including* Dread Naught but Time *and* Stay Awhile: Scenes from Temecula Valley.

Trond is an Associate Artist at Dorland Mountains Arts; Board Secretary for the Temecula Valley Writers and Illustrators non-profit; and owner of the Very Small Press, Trer Publishing.

The Mysterious Smile

by Paulene Turner

In a home-made laboratory, in the backyard of my parents' house, I stare at an empty bench and hold my breath. My dark hair is disheveled, I know, and my eyes have a wild, watery look about them which goes well with the stubble breaking through my pale skin. But I don't care.

"How much longer do we have to wait?" Sasha is impatient.

"Shhhh," I say, my gaze fixed on the bench.

She huffs but keeps the video recording as we focus on the empty space, awaiting a miracle.

And then, with no fanfare or rippling of the air, not even a technological "ting," a honey-colored teddy bear is sitting where nothing was before.

"So, it's 6.29 on 15th April, the year 2035. I'm Milo De Luca, twenty-seven years old, from Sydney, Australia. This is Eddie—" I hold up the toy "—and he's the first bear to travel through time."

Sasha pops her blonde head in front of the camera, joy swimming in her sea-blue eyes. "You did it, Milo! And I witnessed it. Sasha Lockhart, also from Sydney, Australia. Should I give my tax file number or something?"

As I press the OFF button on the camera, Sasha launches herself at me and we hug and bounce around, wild with excitement. I break free to retrieve a bottle of champagne from the lab fridge—Moet et Chandon, purchased especially for this moment.

Popping the cork, a tide of golden liquid fizzes over my hand as I fill two champagne flutes.

"To how many years of research paying off?" Sasha asks, seizing a glass.

"Too many." I sigh.

In truth, I've worked tirelessly since I was seventeen, facing setback after setback in my quest to conquer the mysteries of Time. Other scientists laughed at my ideas, calling me "a dreamer" and a "weekend Bunsen burner." I may not have PhDs like them and I'm not a member of any top science institutes; I'm self-taught, self-funded, and motivated. But now, I'll have the last laugh because I've proved them all wrong.

Sasha holds the Time and Space Machine, which resembles a mobile phone with colorful lights pulsing on its screen, considering its weight. "Weird to think *this* can transport you through time."

"And space," I add. The most important part, so I can explore time zones outside of Sydney, or even Australia.

I take a minute to look around the laboratory in quiet tribute. The test tubes are lined up like scholars. Scribbled calculations and clock doodles cover the walls and the paper around my work bench. Library shelves sag with well-thumbed scientific volumes.

Have I really done it? It hardly seems real. I feel light-headed and dizzy.

"I'm not sure I should drink too much of this—" I hold up the glass "—after no sleep for forty-eight hours."

"Seventy-two," Sasha corrects me. "But who's counting?"

We take our drinks out to the backyard, edged by colorful flowers. Sinking onto the grass, we sip as we watch a glorious suburban sunset.

"To my friend, and the cleverest man who ever lived," says Sasha.

"I can't claim to be the cleverest. There was—" and here, she joins in: "—da Vinci."

"Or Leo, the God, as we call him," she says, jumping up and gesturing theatrically. "Not just a painter, but an inventor, a visionary. He invented the helicopter, the parachute, the tank. And a multi-colored cocktail at my local bar, for which I am truly grateful. How did a man from the Middle Ages dream up all these things? How? How?"

I can't help laughing. "Am I so very boring?"

"On some subjects. Not all." She moves closer, as if about to whisper a secret, and her lips graze my cheek. "Not to me." Backlit by the sun, her expression infused with a tired beyond exhaustion, she's never looked more beautiful to me.

"I couldn't have done it without my brilliant assistant," I say.

"Is that all?"

"And friend?"

She raises an eyebrow, inviting more.

"My sweet love."

Sasha has worked for me for the past nine months, but the latest development in our relationship is still quite new. Neither of us knows where it's going. I just know I want it to keep on going.

As she leans her head on my shoulder, we savor the sour beverage and the sweet moment of triumph.

"The question now," she says, "is are you going to call the Science Society, or shall I? Or we could go and tell them in person, so I can film the smiles slipping off their smug bastard faces."

"Not yet," I say. "They won't believe us. They'll say we doctored that video."

"Well, you can do it again. Send Teddy off and back once more."

I shake my head. "No. Now we need a human trial. If I achieve that, they'll have to see the possibilities."

"Which human? You?" Sasha is aghast. "That would be dangerous."

"Which is why I can't ask anyone else to do it."

"Can I come with you?" she asks.

"Out of the question. Calibrating the journey for one will be difficult enough. And I can't risk you. You're too important to me."

Sasha runs her index finger around the rim of the glass, watching the golden bubbles slowly rise to the surface and burst. "And what about us?" she says. Her gaze dissects me like a scalpel. "You said we had to press pause until you achieved this. But after that, you'd take time out."

"And I will," I reply. "As soon as I return from this trip... and I've written up my research." *And made this year's science grant applications.*

I reach for her hand, but she pulls away, draining her glass. "So where will you go for the first trip through time?"

I feel my cheeks stretch into a grin. *Is that even a question?* I know exactly where I'll go. I've always known. I'll visit *Him*. My hero.

Leonardo da Vinci.

◈

A few days later, I'm ready to leave. Chugging down a half-glass of sauvignon blanc for courage, I take some deep breaths and press *INITIATE TRAVEL.*

Instantly, I'm in a tube of light, ringed by swirling white mist, stretching to infinity. Inside, it's cold and everything shudders, like a plane in rough skies. Crashes and bangs beyond the walls unnerve me. But it's the voices, haunting and troubled, crying out through the fog that almost make me press *RETURN TO TIME AND PLACE OF ORIGIN.* The machine lurches and begins to spin, for so long, so fast, I black out.

◈

Florence, 1477

Returning to consciousness, a scent of cheap spirits and turpentine fills my nostrils. Voices, muffled at first, shape themselves into words.

"Have you got ants wriggling in your pants?" A man's voice, croaky and deep. "Sit still, woman. Unless you want me to paint you a nose the size of the Duomo."

"You try sitting still for a few minutes," a woman replies, nasal and whiny. "It's impossible. Like lice are crawling over your skin. In this dump, they probably are. I don't know why I agreed to do this."

"Because I paid you, Love." The man is speaking in Italian, I realize, which I'm fluent in. "It's more than you'd get serving plonk at your father's tavern."

I'm still a tad dizzy as I stand up and see... a dark-haired woman on a sofa, posing for a portrait, painted by a long-haired man with his back to me. The man stabs his brush at the canvas like he's trying to hurt it.

Spotting me, the woman's sullen expression morphs to a grin. And she throws her head back in a kookaburra cackle.

"What is so funny?" the painter asks, hands on hips. "Have you been at your father's spirits again?"

"And what if I have?" the woman snaps back. "If I'm to spend time in this drafty den, I need a little warmth in my belly."

"As long as that's all you've got in there."

She doesn't hear the last part; she's tipping sideways to see me. "There's a man behind you."

The painter spins around, his dark eyes sweeping up and down me. "You're not due for another hour."

It's around now I notice two things. One, that I'm completely naked. Time travel evidently preserves the body but not the clothes you travel in. And two, the painter looks familiar. He's younger, more unkempt, and smellier than I imagined, but he's uncannily like...

"Leonardo! When can I see the painting?" the woman whines.

Leonardo?

"Patience, Lisa. When I'm done, not before."

"That's not fair."

"Stop your moaning!"

Moaning... Lisa? What?

And now I study the part-finished canvas upon the easel, the work is *really* familiar in dimension and outline. Though not in detail. It portrays a dark-haired woman with a lascivious grin in a gaudily colored hat.

Ohmigod! This is Leonardo da Vinci. And he's painting the *Mona Lisa*. But not as we know it.

"Anyway, I'm done for today." Lisa stands up, readjusting her clothes. "You can stay, sir." She winks at me. "Don't burden yourself with garments on my account."

"I paid for an hour, Lisa! You owe me a drink. Several!" Leonardo shouts as she descends the wooden stairs.

He hurries to a desk, scribbles something on a scrap of paper, wraps it round a rock—one of many he keeps in a bowl—and hurls it out of the window.

"Oh, that's very mature!" Lisa screeches from the street below. "And by the way, you missed!"

Leonardo paces, muttering: "I need something to more accurately knock sense into empty heads." His lips twist to the side as he withdraws a notebook from his artist's gown and scrawls something within.

"I suppose you're an artist too?" he says, joining me at the easel. "You can't trip over a drunk in the street these days without him being a practitioner of fine arts."

"I paint a little," I reply. Then, recalling who I'm talking to: "But I wouldn't call myself an artist. Not like you, Mr. da Vinci."

Leonardo's bottom lip curls as he examines the painting. "Perhaps I could use a novice's eye to tell me what's wrong with this painting."

What's wrong with it? Everything. To start with, he wasn't meant to paint it for another thirty years.

"Have you something I can..." I gesture to my naked form.

Leonardo points to a cupboard in the corner, containing a pile of soiled clothing. I reel back at the smell as I pull on some dark brown leggings and a loose green tunic, sleeves puffed to the elbow, before returning to the artwork. "Well, the model's smile is a bit..." *clown-like and obscene* "... too much," I venture.

"Too much?" Leonardo's right eyebrow pings up in artistic pique but, as he assesses the painting, the pair realign. "You may have a point."

"And the colors are very bright. I wonder how it might look if it was a little more... smoky and mysterious."

"Smoky and mysterious?" Leonardo scratches his chin, then pulls out the notebook and scrawls something in it. I try to see what, but he whips the book back with a furtive air.

"What's your name, sir?"

"Milo. De Luca." My gaze strays to the paintings on the walls. Religious paintings with mother and baby in vibrant colors. Angels, with bird-like wings, birds with human faces. Renderings of the human form with words painted over them: *Boring; Bring Me Something New; Not another nude.*

"Don't look at those," says Leonardo. "Rubbish. I keep them to reuse the canvases."

At the side is a triptych of a debauched-looking dinner party. Again, the form is familiar though the details so strange, it's like I haven't just traveled through time, but to a parallel universe.

"Oh, that was a dinner I attended—" Leonardo waves it away "—where some fellow artists and I resolved to get out of the art business and take real jobs. It was supposed to be our last night in the profession."

"Like a last supper?" My voice cracks.

"Yes."

"And by a real job, you mean...?"

"Tanner, cobblestone-maker, gongfermor?"

Gongfermor? Who empties barrels in castle privies? Leonardo da Vinci? For a moment, I forget how to breathe and clutch the wall to stop from falling.

"But painting's not all I do," Leonardo says. "I'm an inventor too."

I exhale as Leonardo points to some designs sketched on board and loose paper piled up on the floor. My hands shake with anticipation as I hold them. *To think I'm about to see da Vinci's first models for his genius creations!*

And then he reveals his first page. It takes a moment to make sense of the lines. Again, the drawings are weirdly familiar, yet utterly foreign. The first, I'm guessing, is his prototype for a helicopter.

"Well, what do you think?" Leonardo asks.

I want to say something—anything—but I have no words. This flying vehicle has a cabin, but instead of propellers, Leonardo has sketched large bird feathers on top.

"It's a flying machine," says Leonardo impatiently, as though anyone with eyes could see that.

"But how would the feathers lift the machine off the ground?"

"You may well ask the birds that same question!" Leonardo says.

I lick my lips and move to the next design. I hold it one way, then the other, then sideways.

"It's a device to transport one from the top of a mountain to the bottom, without bodily harm," Leonardo offers.

A parachute? An early version. Very, *very* early. I draw my cheeks into a smile, like curtains opening in a theatre. The design includes a harness for a human to lie horizontally, with giant fairy wings on their back.

"How do the wings work?"

"The wind," Leonardo says. I wait for more explanation but there is none, though I catch him squinting at the drawing as if searching for further clues himself.

"I see," I say. Though I've never felt more like a blind man stumbling in a dark cave.

"These days, you can't just be an artist," Leonardo adds. "You need to have a second talent. I'm trying out 'inventor.' If that doesn't succeed, I could become a 'court scoundrel.' That works for some."

I'm taut with trepidation as I prepare to look at the third design. One of his more forward-thinking inventions was the army tank. This is a version of that, I believe. (Though it's not certain.)

It's a giant metal horse.

"Those Greeks had a lot of luck with the Trojan horse. Why not us?" he says.

I can't see wheels on the device, but rather a long string, as if it's meant to be pulled by someone. *A giant, perhaps?*

"Hmmm. Interesting."

"I've heard that said before. 'Interesting!'" Leonardo folds his arms, pouting. "You think I'm crazy."

"No, no, no, no, nooooo. Not at all."

I just can't understand how someone with no practical sense of, well, anything, could become the brilliant inventor hailed across the centuries.

As Leonardo prepares his next canvas, I take the opportunity to look around me. The apartment is small and cramped, overlooking a cobbled street. Rough wooden floor, candles on the wall, a wooden bench with soiled blanket for his models. And canvases everywhere, piled up, hung up, side by side, end to end. Two bowls sit on his artist's desk: one filled with rocks and the other with jewelry—gold rings, earrings, bracelets.

Then I notice, beside his paints, unattended... Leonardo's notebook. I lick my lips. His notebooks are legend. He never went anywhere without one. He sketched everything that interested him and jotted down all his thoughts and ideas. While he's preparing the next canvas, I snatch up the book and flick through, hoping to glimpse the spark that will fire up the foremost mind of science and art.

What do I see? Doodles of birds, like children's cartoons. Lots of expletives, in artistic lettering. And sketches of men and women's private parts, captioned crudely. *A dingly fit for a duchess. What is this thing called, Love? Madam, put that thing down; you know where it's been!* Once again, I feel like I've tripped over my expectations and landed in a bucket of vomit.

I flick to the back page of the notebook and see a list of items. *1 X ring, Signor de Vetchi, 2 X earring Signora Malvolio, 1 X bracelet, Signora Collette Luteci,* and so on. Glancing over at the jewelry bowl, I see a ring with *MV* engraved upon it. Is this an inventory of items received in payment for portraits? *Or something else?*

Leonardo snatches the book from me.

"Sorry. I, err..."

"Well, then... bring out Signor di Giovanni." He gestures to my trousers.

I hesitate, unsure of his meaning. Leonardo leans in. "Lose the leggings, Luigi. Time to show the world what you're made of."

"Oh, I'm not a model." I laugh nervously.

"Then who the hell are you? Turning up here without a stitch on? Were you and I...?" Leonardo tilts his head, eyebrows raised in question.

"No." My face warms. "I'm an admirer. Of your *work*." I add the last part quickly.

"You admire *my* work?" Leonardo regards me with suspicion. "You're a spy, aren't you? That Michelangelo is always trying to find out what I'm up to."

"No!"

"How did you get in here without me hearing you?"

"I don't know. I think I had too much—" *what would they drink here?* "—wine? And woke up over there."

Leonardo glances at the space where I first appeared and back at me, his eyes narrowing. "On your way, then."

"Nice to meet you," I say. I take a last look around, then head down the stairs.

"Wait," Leonardo calls as I'm halfway down. He draws the curtain of hair out of his eyes. "I would like to paint you sometime. You have something about you, Milo De Luca."

I flush with satisfaction, from my crown to my big toe. *Leonardo* remembers *my* name.

❖

Out on the street, the cool air hits me like a bucket of ice. Which I need. I feel muzzy and over-heated with shock and disbelief.

Was that *the* Leonardo da Vinci? Or could it be another artist with the same name? And if it was *Him*, how did he go from *that* misguided, uninspired Leonardo to the one I knew—the Visionary, a household name even hundreds of years hence?

The cobbled street is narrow between the rickety two-story wooden buildings. The only light comes from candlelight spilling from the windows and starlight reflecting on the (suspiciously wet) cobbles. My gaze snags on something white in the darkness: a piece of paper—the one Leo threw out of the window.

My breath hitches as I snap it up. I try to read the writing. HCNEW. There are some letters I recognize—W and H—but the others seem like some strange language, or... they're written backwards. *Of course!* Leonardo was famous for backwards writing—mirror language—to protect his ideas. My overtaxed brain is slow to process the letters. *WENCH.* I presume it's intended as derision. An insult from Leonardo to Lisa. *The* Mona Lisa.

I look up at the window to find Leonardo watching me, half in, half out of the shadows, before he withdraws once more into the darkness.

"Hey! You with the nice legs!"

I look around to find Lisa in the doorway of a bar, The Rose and Thistle, waving me in. "Come have a glass of wine."

"I don't have any money to pay," I say.

"Leo didn't pay you?" She tuts and shakes her head. "Never mind, we'll do what I do whenever he tries to cheat me. We'll put it on his bill."

I follow her into the bar. And to be clear, I'm following "the moaner, Lisa" into Leonardo da Vinci's local drinking establishment. Where he is going to pay for my drink. Lisa goes behind the bar and pours me a cup of red wine from a ceramic cask.

"Saluti!" she says.

It's crowded tonight, with men in long tunics over leggings. Sawdust is sprinkled around the floor, casks of wine sit on the wooden service counter. A pig runs after a chicken. Just your average Renaissance bar.

Lisa, serving the all-male clientele, is something to behold. She chides this one, laughs loudly, lewdly, with that one, and turns another out, with a take-no-prisoners air. She's a vibrant woman of many colorful moods, but none of them—at least while I'm watching—are contemplative or understated. I witness big broad smiles, dark thunderous brows, but not a single half-smile to drive a world crazy for hundreds of years. So where did that come from?

I rub Leonardo's note between my fingers, feeling its solidity to assure myself that this is real; I really am here. Maybe I could present it to the Science Society as proof of my journey. They'd test it, find the paper was made in the 1400s. I could get Sasha to film the shock and awe on their faces.

Sasha. I sip my wine and take a moment to think about my "girlfriend." Well, not officially mine, yet—I couldn't make a commitment like that until I'd completed my work. But hopefully, she soon will be.

I call up a memory of her dancing on the lawn, her intelligent eyes, her perfect teeth. Her blonde, wavy hair catching the sunlight, like it was on fire, like a painting. A Botticelli. *The Birth of Venus*. Sasha has been patient, taking a back seat to my work, my obsession. But she deserves more, and when I get back, I'll give her my full attention. We could even take a holiday somewhere? Florence, perhaps?

"You're a thief!" An old man leaps to his feet, fists raised at Lisa. "One minute I had a full glass and the next it's half empty."

"Sit down, Marco," Lisa commands, laughing indulgently. "It's just the way with drink. There's not a man in this room who will disagree. Nor a woman, for that matter. We ladies keep hoping you men have a full vessel, but it usually runs dry well before our thirst is quenched."

Everyone dissolves into bawdy chuckling, including the complainer. Lisa looks over at me and winks.

I spot something at the end of the bar, a strange-looking broom, with a leather belt strapped to the top. "Excuse me, what's that?" I ask as Lisa passes by.

"That's Leo's latest invention," she says. "He says if I strap the broom around my waist, it can sweep up behind me as I go."

That was one of Leonardo's inventions? My face must have betrayed my thoughts, because she raises her eyebrows and nods. "Loony Leo comes up with something new every week."

"L-l-loony Leo?" I can hardly get the words out.

She points to another of his inventions. A wooden sculpture dangling from the ceiling, likes a child's mobile, with three fish: big fish, mouth agape, medium fish, and little fish. As you twirl it around, the big fish eats the medium fish, who devours the smaller one.

"Clever," I say. Lisa nods and leans in conspiratorially. "After a few drinks, we draw our patrons' attention to it. And while they're gawping, we pour half their drink back into the barrel. So, they have to buy more."

What the—? Could Leonardo da Vinci have made that cute sculpture for such a grubby, mercantile purpose?

"He's devious, that one." Lisa taps her nose. "Watch yourself around him. He's not called 'light-fingered Leo' for nothing. Your coin and jewels are not safe when he's nearby. The man's been known to pay his bill with rings and gold from his rich, foolish clients and not-so-rich local inebriates."

My mind flashes to his desk and the bowl filled with jewelry. Were those pieces stolen? Surely not!

They say you should never meet your heroes. I'm not sorry I met Leo, but certain aspects have been... disappointing. He's definitely slipped from God to mere mortal status for me, with the emphasis on mere.

And then... I have a sense, for the second time today, of freefalling through space. I gasp and pat myself down as I realize, with horror, I don't have the time machine on me. I'm not even sure where it is. Presumably I had it in my hands when I arrived. I must have dropped it while I slept, somewhere in Leonardo's studio.

◆

I take off at speed, stumbling over the uneven cobbles in the dark, splashing through a puddle reeking of urine. I take the stairs to Leonardo's loft two at a time. A naked man is bent over, head in the cupboard. When he turns to look at me, his face is trenched with confusion.

"Where's Leonardo?" I ask.

"I wondered the same thing." He scratches his head volubly. "He was sketching me in an Atlas pose, you know, holding up the world. And then, he squatted down over there behind the canvases. I heard him make a few "Ahhh" sounds and he was gone. Just. Disappeared. I thought he might have slipped downstairs, but I don't see how. I was just checking the cupboard, in case it was some kind of trick. But he's not there."

His voice is a background drone, drowned out by my ragged breathing as I search the floor in and around the pile of canvases and sketches of ridiculous inventions to find... nothing at all. I check and recheck every inch of Leo's loft, even places I haven't been (like the privy! Ooh! Don't get me started!). But it's nowhere. The time machine is gone.

And I know who has it. *Light-fingered Leo.*

I sink to the ground, head in my hands, reeling with the desperation of my situation.

"Are you alright?" the model asks.

No, I'm pretty far from alright. I'm stuck here, in this time. Possibly for the rest of my life. I know no-one, except Lisa. I have no idea how to live here. I think of my lab, the familiar smell of burnt chemicals, the colorful spines of books in the library. I'll never see them again. Or my family.

Or Sasha. The thought of losing her, and her smile, and her laughter like wind chimes, before we've really even begun, stabs my chest so hard I find myself clawing at my collar.

"Of course he's okay," a familiar voice answers. "Aren't you, Milo?"

A hand appears before me to help me to my feet. Leonardo's. He looks neater and smells of aftershave—Dior, if I'm not mistaken. His hair is still long but shiny and groomed, like it's been washed and blow-dried. He's wearing the same shirt he had on earlier, but it's paired with black denim jeans. *My jeans.*

As our eyes meet, I know. His smug grin confirms it.

"You can go," he tells the model. "I don't feel like drawing right now."

The protest on the boy's lips dies as Leonardo holds up some coins. The boy grabs them, pulls on some clothes, and gallops downstairs. All the while, Leo and I hold the eye lock.

"Where's my time machine?" I demand.

"It's here. Unharmed."

He holds it up and I snatch it. "You had no right to take it."

"Many apologies," he says, and bows. "You are, truly, a genius, sir."

That appeases me a tad. *Leonardo* thinks *I'm* a genius. "What did you think of the future?"

"I saw creatures in strange clothes, and cities of such impressive scale and design. And some Netflix series. One about me."

"How long were you there?" I ask.

"A month," he says. "I did consider staying longer. Permanently, even. But this is my home. And I have a lot of work to do."

He looks with distaste around the room. "Though I'm not staying in this chicken coop for much longer. There's a nice little estate in the Tuscan hills I have my eye on."

So, he's returned richer than when he departed?

"Steal anything while you were there?" I ask, my voice acid.

He chuckles. "I did acquire a few keepsakes."

Acquire? "And some ideas, I suppose? Inspiration for your inventions? Your art?"

"Well, we'll see," Leonardo says cryptically. "Time will tell."

From his self-satisfied air, I can tell he's taken all he needs to become the person he will be. I'm not sure why it annoys me as much as it does, as he's only stealing from himself. Or is he?

"But I would advise you to get going soon, my friend," Leo says. "The power source on the machine is dangerously low. I wasn't sure how to boost it up. Nor was your assistant."

"My assistant? You mean Sasha?"

"I call her Alexandra, but yes..." The way he says her name, in this oily, pretentious fashion, incenses me.

"You didn't do anything to her, did you?"

"Well, I know things are more 'open' in the future, but in this time, a gentleman does not kiss and tell."

He tips his head and a broad, overconfident smile breaks out, like the plague, on his face, which I really *really* want to hit just now.

"To return, you just have to press RETURN TO—"

"*I* know how to operate *my* machine, thank you." My tone is flinty enough to set the room alight. I glance down then and notice Leo's boots. They're mine, too. My favorite pair. I imagine I might see them in Leo's self-portraits in future.

One thing confuses me. "How did you arrive back here with your clothes intact?" My garments had evaporated during the journey.

"Alexandra helped me make a minor adjustment to the time-spin ratio. That seemed to work."

He has a dreamy look as he mentions Sasha again. *How dare you!* I want to say. And a lot more besides. But I'm keen to get going on the journey home, to fix anything that needs fixing. I satisfy myself with a final glare, before I press RETURN TO PLACE AND TIME OF ORIGIN.

As I blast off, I hear him shouting. "Thank you! So much! What a month! Arrivederci, mi amico!" He laughs. A resonant and sinister laugh that seems to echo through the mist all the way home.

Eventually, the spinning begins, and, though I try to resist, I fall unconscious.

❖

When I awake, I'm back in my laboratory. It's a month after my departure.

I give a cry of excitement, checking everything is as I left it. Some science equipment is gone, a few books are missing—one of my favorite works on da Vinci, among them. Plus, a ring of onyx and gold my parents gave me for my 21st birthday. I know where that will be now—in a bowl, in a Florentine loft, with the rest of the stolen loot. I know, too, that when I inspect my wardrobe, a pair of my jeans will be missing and some boots. I wonder what else Leo took while he was here.

On my lab bench is a note in a strange hand. The letters are half backwards. das ooT, daB ooT. *Mirror writing.*

I'm about to check it in the glass when I hear behind me, "Leonardo, do you fancy a break? We could have an aperitif..."

Seeing me, Sasha stops, open-mouthed. She looks me up and down, taking in the dank tunic and leggings, before launching herself into my arms. I embrace her too but can't help thinking about that flicker of disappointment in her eyes when she saw it was me. Not *Him.*

"So, the time machine really works?" she says.

"Yes, it does. And I'm guessing you met Leonardo?"

"Leo the God? Yes, I did."

"God no more. Just a person, and a flawed one like the rest of us," I say.

"He won't be back then?"

"Not if I can help it."

She nods and smiles but a tautness around the jaw hints at disappointment.

"What's that?" She points to the note in my hand.

"It's from Leonardo." She snatches it from me, squinting at it. "Where's a mirror?"

I point to a small glass near the sink. We bump heads as we clamor to inspect it. "Too bad, Too sad," I read.

What does he mean by that?

"Was Leonardo everything you hoped he'd be?" Sasha asks.

"No." I sigh. "He didn't really live up to expectations."

She twirls her hair and smiles. "In some ways, maybe not. In others..."

For a moment, she seems lost in her own secret musings. And when she looks up at me again, she has this look—a half-smile that is mysterious and smoky and way too familiar.

And I know... what else he took from me.

About the Author

Paulene Turner is the writer of the six-book YA series The Time Travel Chronicles *and* Heartbeats, *a collection of short stories linked by sub-plots of love. She has worked as a journalist in Australia and the UK. She also writes and directs short plays for Short and Sweet, Sydney.*

Find out more about her work at www.pauleneturnerwrites.com

LET'S TACO 'BOUT LOVE

BY NORA FRY

Most girls binge on a few pints of ice cream after a nasty breakup, but not Rosa De la Cruz. Rosa bought an ice cream truck.

The salesman had coughed, rubbing the back of his neck. "Uh... just so you know, this baby doesn't go in reverse anymore."

A dilapidated food truck wasn't part of her *very detailed* five-year plan—color-coded spreadsheets, investment goals, all of it—but her ex had already stolen her savings *and* her sense of direction. Selling the little Honda her mamá gave her for graduation was the only way to fund what was left of her future.

Rosa ran a hand over the sun-faded paint, ignoring the frayed seat cushions and lingering scent of turmeric. "That's fine," she said, handing over the money. "I'm not planning on looking back."

Pulling into her parents' circular driveway, Rosa could feel the heat coming from her mother's glare all the way across the yard. Rosa winced. Instead of parking the sporty little red Honda, Rosa sat behind the wheel of a golden-yellow truck emblazoned with *What's Your Curry?*

Mamá's chanclas slapped the pavement as she stomped back toward the house. The bang of the screen door punctuated her outrage.

Rosa walked slowly up the driveway toward the still-swinging door. Mutters rose above the thwack of a knife on the cutting board.

"Two years! *Two years* I saved my pennies to buy her that car, and what does she do? One little breakup and—poof!—it's gone, just like that thieving manchild! And now she thinks she can run away from her problemas in that piece of junk *trastajo*!" The knife slammed down. "What's next—cutting off all her beautiful hair?"

Rosa sucked in a deep breath, pasted on her old beauty pageant smile, and stepped into the cozy lion's den—a riot of terracotta, turquoise, and temper.

"Not run away, Mamá! Drive away! I'm going to use Abuela's recipes and run an ice cream truck. Mmm... are you making horchata?"

Mamá waved her knife at Rosa. "Don't try to change the subject, mija! If your abuela knew about this, she'd climb out of her grave and wear out your hide with a chancla herself. You can't fix everything wrong in your life with ice cream."

"Maybe not with grocery store ice cream, but Abuela's homemade helado should do the trick."

Mamá punched buttons and yelled over the howling blender.

"So, my brilliant Ivy League Rosa is going to be like that Juan guy who drives around blaring mariachi?"

Rosa wasn't about to admit it to Mamá, but hearing taco truck mariachi music drifting from the used auto lot had planted a seed of inspiration. She glanced at the grease-spotted bags on the counter and raised a brow. "If people buy half as many of my ice creams as you do his tacos, I'll be rich."

She pursed her lips, tapped her chin, and sang out the flavors Mamá could never resist: "*Dulce de Leche Swirl... Mango con Chile...* maybe even *Coconut con Cajeta*?"

Mamá's scream drowned out the blender. Rosa escaped with her life, a spicy pork taco, and Mamá's favorite scrub brush.

After several weeks of scrubbing curry from every corner of the truck (and her hair), planning routes, perfecting the paintwork, and testing abuela-inspired flavors on eager cousins, Rosa was ready.

Despite countless calls to auto shops and a parade of "just stop by and we'll take a look," she still couldn't check *fix the reverse issue* off her spreadsheet. Putting it there in the first place had been her parents' idea, not hers. One deeply regrettable YouTube tutorial might have made things worse, but she wasn't about to let a little thing like not being able to go in reverse stop her from moving forward.

Just before lunchtime, she pulled her freshly painted pink-and-turquoise truck into the lot between the city park and the library. Sliding her serving window open, Rosa grinned at the squeals of delight from the kids around the park: "¡Helado! ¡Mamá! An ice cream truck!"

Rosa chuckled as a staff member scurried out of the library, set up a "NO outside food or drink" sign, and then promptly bought the first bowl—a two-scoop *Mango con Chile.*

As she scooped and served bowl after bowl, Rosa's mind danced with sweet possibilities—chocolate-dipped waffle cones, cold drinks, and other indulgent additions felt tantalizingly within reach.

Rosa's daydreams were cut short as the happy jingle of her truck was drowned out by trumpets and guitars. From around the corner, she saw it—clouds of black exhaust trailing behind a dingy yellow taco truck, which had the nerve to park right in front of hers. Her shiny truck vanished in a haze of fumes. Cinnamon-sugar and tacos battled with the pong of burnt oil.

Coughing and waving her arms, Rosa didn't even need to look: *Wanna Taco 'Bout It?* was plastered across the side in bold purple letters.

Rosa's grip on her ice cream scoop tightened. No, she did not want to talk about it—not now, not ever, and certainly not when that yellow truck was poised to steal every sniff, every customer, every scrap of attention her poor little ice cream truck could claim.

She'd seen it, had been part of it. Mamá's street was right on his summer route. Juan Ramirez-Espero's taqueria-on-wheels blasted mariachi from dawn to dinner. Every time he stopped, parents came running, money in hand.

As the exhaust dispersed, the mouthwatering scent of roasting meat drifted across the parking lot, making her stomach churn. Even she couldn't resist his pork carnitas—her money practically danced out of her wallet every time he passed.

Sliding open the windows, Juan hollered, "Churros! Carnitas! You know you want 'em!" People cheered. Rosa growled, but then again, so did her stomach.

Gathering her courage, Rosa strode up to Juan's truck window. She left her wallet behind. She was intent on giving him a piece of her mind—not a piece of her hard-earned cash.

"What's your problem? You have the whole west side of the park unoccupied, and you park right next to my food truck. Can't you find somewhere else to give people diarrhea?"

Juan stopped stacking napkins by the pickup window. "Hey now, señorita, it's still a free country, isn't it?" He leaned against the counter, flashing her an easy smile. "Us food trucks gotta stick together."

Rosa fought the childish urge to stamp her foot. "By 'sticking together,' you mean nearly nicking my fender and coating my fresh paint in soot from your smoke-belching wreck?"

Juan patted the roof fondly. "Sorry about that. She gets a little smoky when I run her on fryer oil. I'm sure I can find some way to make it up to you, Miss?"

"Rosa." She practically spat the word at him.

"Well, Rosa, it's nice to meet you, though I feel like we've met before, no?" His eyes narrowed in thought, lips curving just a little. "Looks like I've got customers coming." He snapped on some gloves. "Excuse me, please—unless you'd like to order?"

Rosa snatched a napkin and stalked off. It was hard to be that close to carnitas and not drool. Her fingers twitched at her empty pocket. Normally, by now, she'd have a plate in hand—extra creamy salsa on the side. Rosa climbed into her truck, cinched her apron, and squared her shoulders. "It's fine," she muttered. "Totally fine." Then she straightened her stacks of bowls, lined up sample spoons, and put on her best pageant smile.

Rosa waited. She watched.

One, two, five, ten customers wandered toward her truck, sniffed the air, and veered straight to Juan's sizzling carnitas. Rosa exhaled sharply. "That thief!" she muttered, gripping the edge of her window like it was the only thing keeping her from launching a scoop at Juan's smiling face.

She opened her register to check her change, blindly shuffling bills as her throat tightened. Was every charming man she met out to steal her dreams?

Then, out of the corner of her eye, Rosa saw him pointing at her—and froze, half expecting another culinary ambush. She raised an eyebrow and forced on a smile as a woman carrying a basket of tacos approached.

"Juan said it's gonna be another ten minutes till the next batch of churros are fried," the woman explained, glancing back at the taco truck. "Told me I should get some of your helado to tide me over."

Rosa blinked. Juan was... sending her customers? Her scoop hovered over the tubs. She squinted at his truck. He caught her eye and smiled, flipping a tortilla onto a sizzling grill.

Her strained smile grew genuine. "Churros? I think I've got something that'll go perfectly with those." Rosa held her breath as the woman dipped a churro into the creamy swirls of *Dulce de Leche* and took a bite. The woman's eyes went wide. "¡Es *mmmazing*!" Rosa laughed when the second dip and bite came even faster. The rave review spread quickly through the crowd, and when the customer came back for seconds, she wasn't alone.

Hours passed, tacos grilled, churros fried, and ice cream melted. Crowds bought churros from Juan, and he sent them over to Rosa's for creamy bowls of helado to dip them in. Grateful, she sent her new customers over to Juan's for churros and tacos, nodding his way. "Seriously, don't pass them up—especially the green chile pork."

Rosa's stomach growled as another customer came up to the window with an overflowing red oval basket from Juan's. Rosa turned her smile up a notch.

"Ice cream to go with those tacos?"

"Juan said to give you this, Miss. Two pork carnitas, extra creamy salsa verde, and pickled jalapeños on the side? Oh, and a horchata with no ice? I didn't even know he sold that, Miss." Rosa's eyes widened as she recognized her favorite order. Juan remembered?

Looking over at Juan's truck, she saw him wiping down his counters, a slight smile on his face—and then he winked. The crackling smoky carnitas tasted like heaven, the spicy tang of jalapeño in the salsa was perfection, and Rosa wished she had more time to savor it—but her line was growing again.

Mid-afternoon, Juan popped up at her order window. "Hey, Rosa, *linda*, I need that basket back. You gonna keep it all day? I mean, if you want a souvenir, I could sign..." Juan's voice trailed off as he caught sight of a framed photo hung on her truck's wall. "Why do you have a photo of Guadalupe De la Cruz?"

"She's my inspiration, *and* my abuela."

"Lupe is your grandmother? She was my first customer! She told me my salsa verde wasn't fit for a dog."

Rosa laughed. "That sounds like Abuela."

Juan chuckled. "Luckily, she took pity on me and gave me her favorite recipe. I owe a lot to that woman."

Rosa's eyes widened. "Are you kidding me? Mamá has wanted that receta for years! Abuela wouldn't give it to her."

A customer yelled, "Hey! Juan! Are you gonna flirt all day or are you gonna sell me some carnitas?"

"Oh, gotta go. We're gonna 'taco' 'bout this more later though!"

As the lines of customers flowed through the day, so did the questions.

"Eh, Rosa! Are you using your abuela's recipes? I still dream of that helado she made for fiestas when I was a kid."

"What? Juan, I'm not telling you that. You've already taken the family salsa recipe, and don't think I didn't notice your horchata tastes a little too familiar. One more recipe and you'll have a monopoly—you could start building hotels!"

"Actually, the horchata recipe is my own, but I'm glad you think it's up to your abuela's standards!"

A few minutes later Juan called as he rapidly prepped in a rare lull. "Rosa! Got any napkins? I ran out. Chopping all these onions really gets the eyes going. Give a guy a break, eh?"

Grinning, Rosa sent a customer back to Juan with a stack of pink napkins. "Better get used to that feeling then, after I tempt all your customers away with my ice cream!"

It was the most exhausting—and exhilarating—day Rosa had had in years, and not a single item on her meticulously organized list had gone according to plan.

Finally, the crowds began heading home. As the sunset swirled the clouds, Rosa noticed a line of ragged figures at Juan's truck. Juan cheerfully greeted each one by name as he gave the local homeless fresh, warm meals.

Rosa scooped the last creamy dabs from her bins into bowls, stacked a tray full, and joined Juan by his truck. Shy protests were met with a smile and a "Por favor, you're helping *me* out! It won't stay good."

Their gratitude was more than worth the cost of a few bowls of ice cream.

One man glanced up as he finished his meal. "You know, you two really make a good combo." Rosa straightened from where she was leaning on Juan's truck. "Oh we're not a—" Rosa blushed as she realized the man was dipping his churro in ice cream. "Right. Those do go great together."

After everyone left, an exhausted Rosa sanitized empty ice cream bins and folded down her awning. She felt deeply satisfied with her efforts today, like she could finally move forward with her life.

Except she couldn't.

Rosa groaned, thumping her head on the door. Of course. Juan's truck was still directly in front of hers. And despite there being plenty of room to back up behind her, her truck didn't go in reverse.

Knocking on the door to her truck, Juan grinned and held out a small bag of warm churros. "Crazy day, eh? You look like you could use a churro. I happen to know where to get some fantastic ones. Got any of that fabulous ice cream left? We could taco load off."

Remembering her predicament, Rosa sighed and absently crunched a churro. "Now's not the time, Juan."

Juan brushed damp curls off his forehead. "What's wrong? I thought we made an excellent team. I helped you. You helped me. We should do this every day! We could make a hel-of-a-lado money."

He grinned, waiting for her to laugh at the silly joke.

Rosa shook her head and busied herself, too embarrassed to look at him. "I really want to go home."

"Well, why don't you?"

"I can't move."

"I've been told I have that effect on women."

"My truck, Juan!" Rosa's cheeks grew hot. "I can't." She groaned and it all burst out. "It doesn't go in reverse... and now I can't move until you do."

"And here I thought you couldn't get away from the smell of good tacos. I actually do have a couple more hours of cleanup still to do around here."

"Juan!" she protested.

"But—" he grinned, drawing out the word "—I suppose I wouldn't want to leave you stranded. How about I make the first move?"

As Rosa's eyes widened, Juan cleared his throat.

"*I mean*, I'll move my truck... after I give you the number of the best mechanic I know."

"Who?"

Juan dug a tattered business card from his wallet that read *Juan Stop Mechanic Shop.* Leaning against her truck, he held it up like a winning poker hand.

"What can I say? Looks like I am the Juan for you."

Juan's cinnamon-sugar grin widened as Rosa choked on a mouthful of churro. Struggling to regain her composure, she dipped it in the ice cream and took another bite.

The warm crunch melted into the creamy sweetness of her helado—a perfect mix of crisp and cold. She savored the flavor and the day: unexpected, unplanned, exhausting, but maybe, just maybe, exactly what she needed.

Looking up, she caught a serious look in his brown eyes. She bumped her elbow against his, pretending to think it over.

"You might be, Juan," she said at last. "You just might be."

About the Author

Nora Fry is a writer, researcher, teacher, mother, wife, friend, introvert, and caretaker to too many animals to count. Her background in research and education shapes her writing with curiosity, precision, and a fondness for questions that resist easy answers.

When she isn't writing, Nora can be found teaching, reading several books at once, tending animals, or disappearing into long conversations about folklore, science, art, and the strange things people believe when no one is watching. Her work has appeared in Outlet Art and Literary Journal, Suddenly... and Without Warning, Artists & Climate Change, The Southern Standard, *and the* Forgetting Something? *short story anthology by PageTurn Press.*

THREE TICKETS TO TELLURIDE

BY NIKKI BLAKELY

DOLLY

It was December 10, 1903, when I boarded the Rio-Grande Western Railroad with Horace's letter tucked neatly into the inside pocket of my petticoat, and his Christmas gift, a heart-shaped ruby brooch, fastened securely at my breast.

My dearest Eliza, the letter read, *I have wonderful news! All my efforts have not been for naught. Last week while mining near Potosi Peak, we were rewarded when we struck a rich vein of silver! At long last, I am finally able to send for you so we may begin our lives together. We are to be very rich indeed! I have secured first-class passage for you to Telluride by railway—come at once! I should like to be married on Christmas Day, if at all possible. Lastly, I enclose an early Christmas gift—a heart for my heart. I do so hope you love it as much as I do you. Eternally yours, Horace.*

I had never met Horace, and neither had my sister, Eliza. They'd started corresponding by post the previous summer, having been introduced by one of Eliza's professors at the university. The letters came regularly, once, twice, sometimes even three times in a week. Oh, how she went on and on—*Horace this* and *Horace that!* It was enough to turn even the strongest stomach.

Only the day prior I found myself home earlier than usual and intercepted the mail before Eliza. The weight and bulk of this particular letter indicated it to be more than just paper and ink. My curiosity aroused, I was immediately holding it over a steaming kettle, loosening the seal. Once opened and read, a bee began to buzz in my bonnet. Why should Eliza be the one to marry well, to live a life of luxury and comfort, while I languished, left to a life of domestication and drudgery, my beauty fading away to nothing, the same fate that had befallen our mother?

According to our father, not only had I inherited my mother's beauty—her porcelain skin, blue eyes, and rosebud lips—but also her predisposition to frivolity, folly, and all other such womanly ailments and shortcomings. Eliza, on the other hand, had inherited his head for numbers. She was his favorite, and they spent many an afternoon in his study, discussing politics, world events, and mathematical theories. She was the son he never had. With her close-set eyes, broad forehead, and weak chin, she certainly looked the part.

By the time they found me out, it would be too late. The marriage would be consummated, and with any luck, I'd already be with child, if I wasn't already. It's true I'd had my pick of beaus, and I'd picked many, and often, the latest being one Georgie Whitmore, who'd promised a ring on my finger but never delivered. As of late, my dresses had begun to tighten about the mid-section, and I feared it only a matter of time before a little Whitmore would make its presence known.

I pocketed the letter and the brooch and sat down to pen my first letter.

My dearest Horace, please forgive my penmanship as my hand trembles so with excitement I can barely keep it still enough to get the words on the page. I will pack my belongings henceforth and leave straight away. You can expect my arrival in two weeks. Yours truly, Eliza.

The next letter I wrote was from Horace to Eliza, his handwriting being not as difficult to duplicate as it was quite womanly, full of flourishes, loops, curlicues, and the like.

Dearest Eliza, I regretfully inform you of my decision to marry another woman. I realized I could not spend the rest of my life looking upon such an uncomely visage as the one you possess, and I did not want a brood of possum-faced nippers running around. I found someone who is more pleasing to the eye than to the intellect. Do not contact me; I will not be changing my mind. P.S.—I hear that no-count Georgie Whitworth is available. No-longer-yours, Horace.

When I boarded the train the next morning, none was the wiser.

JASPER

I lingered at the bar near the dining car, just out of view, sipping my Kentucky Straight, waiting for the sign from the Girl. Two hours had come and went, but still her hat remained perched on her head as if it had all the time in the world. I was vexed she was taking so long, but this was not unusual for her. She took her time, but she always got it right, unlike the others before her, who often got it wrong.

The Girl, and I called them all that—not because I couldn't remember their names—well, maybe I couldn't. They all looked the same: small, birdlike, and bony with big, sorrowful eyes that followed you everywhere you went. The main reason I called them *Girl,* even to their faces, was that it made the doing of what had to be done later... well, easier.

This particular Girl I found just outside of Tallahassee, painting portraits on the back of playing cards, charging a quarter each. She called them *portraits miniatures,* said the words with a French accent—*oooh fancy*—as if they were something other than what they really were, just another skin game. Her Pa had died, she'd said... blah blah blah. I'd heard it a thousand times before from every other Girl that came before her. If there was a dead father in the picture, they were ripe for the picking, falling outta the trees almost.

I used this Girl same as the others. First, I'd spot the mark, then the Girl would lure them in, vouch for my trustworthiness, my upstanding nature. Next, I'd find out what ailed them. Something *always* ailed them, and whatever it was, I had just the fix. Any one of my magic elixirs, extracts, or cure-all tonics would do the trick. And the trick was, all the potions were the same: a tincture made from colloidal silver and laudanum. Whatever I'd sell them, and they *always* bought, would (usually) be enough to knock them out for the night. Then the Girl would go in and rifle their belongings unnoticed, taking whatever valuables could be found.

Then there was a second use for the Girl. I would get her started on the tonic straightaway. She too had ailments, didn't she? *Who didn't?* Once hooked, she'd do whatever I wanted. The wealthy gentlemen on board, the ones who wouldn't dream of stepping foot into a brothel, had no problem paying a pretty penny for a quick tussle in a private compartment while the Missus was otherwise occupied. And at last, when the Girl had outlived her usefulness, and she *always* did, I would sell her to the closest cathouse. Then wait patiently for the next one to fall from a tree.

This particular Girl had proved her usefulness beyond the usual. It was her idea to do the before-and-after photographs. We'd buy them from a local photographer. They were no one we knew, just random folk, the uglier and worse off the better. Then the Girl would "fix" the photographs with her painting skills. One poor fella, a large portly man with a goiter hanging off his neck, dead in the eyes, and balding; in the after photo, not only was the goiter gone, but he'd have miraculously lost thirty pounds, his complexion cleared, grown both a full head of hair and a renewed sex drive (you could tell the latter by the slight smile on his face that had not been there before). Since we'd incorporated the before-and-after photos, my sales had quadrupled.

One problem though, thus far. This Girl had refused to partake of the tonic. Said it interfered with her painting, But I wasn't too concerned since I now had the contraptions to consider.

Potions were a thing of the past; contraptions were the way of the future. But not just any old kind of contraption. The electrified kind. The Manipulator and the Health Jolting Chair had been around for years, but the new electrified versions, now they were something! They plugged directly into a lamp socket and gave a stimulating, electrical vibration while using them. All I needed was a wealthy investor or two, and I wouldn't even need the potions anymore.

In Oklahoma City, the demonstration of the chair had not gone as planned due to some faulty wiring, but that was all fixed now. And with any luck, tonight's demonstration in the dining car would be just the ticket to secure the funds I needed. After that, I'd have no use for the Girl; she could go back to her street corner and paint portraits on playing cards.

I was so caught up in my reverie I hadn't noticed the Girl was giving the sign; the hat had finally come off and she was waving it impatiently in the air.

"Jasper, there you are," she said as I sauntered up, rolling my suitcase of wares behind me. "I'd like you to meet my new friend, Eliza."

"Jasper W. Mucklebee, at your service." I gave a slight bow before sliding into the vacant seat beside the Girl.

"How do," Eliza replied. "You're a salesman?"

"No, indeed, not a salesman. I'm an entrepreneur."

Eliza looked alarmed. "Well, I, sir, am a Presbyterian. I'm not sure I should be consorting with the likes of an 'En-Tree-Preeno ur.'"

"Oh, my dear, not to fret. An entrepreneur is just another name for Presbyterian. Now, I can't help but notice that beautiful ruby brooch you're wearing. It's stunning. I don't believe I've ever seen anything quite like it before."

"No sir, it is one of a kind, special made. A wedding gift from my fiancé," Eliza said, beaming. "We're to be married on Christmas Day."

"Well then, congratulations are in order! But tell me, how do you do otherwise? Do you have any aches, pains, or ailments? No, don't tell me, let me guess. Perhaps a touch of hysterics? A wandering womb? I've just the ticket for that, a little apparatus known as 'the Manipulator.' Perhaps you're familiar? My version is electrified, much improved over the older hand-cranked version. When applied to the nether regions, it is most invigorating. I can offer you a free demonstration if you'd like. Privately, of course."

"I'm sure I don't know what you mean." Eliza blushed.

"Oh, I'm sure you do." I winked at her. "But at any rate, if that's not what ails you, I'm sure we can find something else."

"Jasper, I was thinking," said the Girl.

"Good for you!"

"Eliza confided in me that her fiancé is a learned man, and during their correspondence by mail, she'd been counseled by her sister on politics, world affairs, and the like. She's worried that when the meetin' time comes, she may not be up to conversating with him in such matters." Here she leaned in and whispered, loud enough for all to hear. "I know I shouldn't have told her about the 'Thinking Tonic,' but you know better than anyone I was dumber than a dodger before I took it, and well, look at me now."

"I told you not to tell anyone!" I said, mock-scornful. "That is our own private supply of Thinking Tonic. We haven't much left."

"I'll pay whatever you ask," Eliza said. "Well, not me. I don't have any money, but my fiancé does. He owns a silver mine in Telluride. He's a very rich man."

"Not to fret, my dear. I'm sure we can work something out. In the meantime, why not have a free sample on the house?" I was no longer thinking of the brooch, but of the chair, and the wealthy investor I needed.

THE GIRL

When Pa up and died from the consumption, and Ma married Henry Scoggins, I couldn't blame her. What else was she to do with all those little'uns to feed? But then I saw the way Henry's look lingered on me just a little longer than it should've; it was the kind of look that should only be seen by a bride on her wedding night. I knew I had to cut and run. Ma and the boys would be fine, and there was nothing for it noways.

I was able to scrape a meager living from the portraits. The hours I'd spent with Pa in his shop, him working on pocket watches and me hunched over a small snippet of paper, painting a portrait to slip into the back side, had paid off. Pa gave me three cents a piece, and while I was inclined to think he got more, I did not mind.

Jasper tried to get me on the tonic straightaway, but I wasn't as stupid as he thunk. He didn't partake himself, but he sure enjoyed his drink, and if there was one thing I'd learnt in all my born days, it was that nothing gets a tongue to waggin' faster than the pulling of a cork. If you listen closely, sometimes you can learn a lot more from what isn't being said than from what is.

When I set to chattin' up the pretty lady with the red brooch, I could tell straight away she was a few cards short. Said her name was Eliza, but everyone called her Dolly and I could see why; she looked just like a china doll and had a head full of air just like. She told me she'd never met her fiancé in person; they'd only conversated by post, and it was her sister who'd helped her write the letters. I put two and two together, but did not see reason to convey these particulars to Jasper.

When she let it spill her fiancé was rich, I could see the cogs a-turnin' in Jasper's thick noggin, and I knew he was thinking about that dang chair of his. He'd planned another demonstration of the thing that very night, so he gave Eliza a taste of the tonic—just enough to make her agreeable, but not enough to buffalo her completely.

During the last demonstration in Oklahoma City, there was a problem with the chair, and Jasper got a bigger jolt than he was expecting. The soles of his shoes started smoking and darn near melted off. This did not impress them potential investors so much, and old Jasper was fit to be tied. Now I'm not saying it was me who crossed those wires, and I'm not saying it wasn't, but somehow after he'd fixed 'em, unbeknownst to him, somehow they got crossed again. Wires got a way of doing that. Pa had once told me that electricity likes to run through silver, so this time, for good measure, I spread a liberal amount of "Thinking Tonic" on the metal footplate. When Jasper's bare feet (he thought it best to remove his shoes since the previous mishap) touched that metal place and he pulled the lever—*Hooo-weee!* His body got all stiff like, his face contorted something awful, and his hair just about stood up on end. The lights in the dining car blinked on and off a few times before shutting off completely, and the vile stink of burnt meat filled the room. All in all, it added three additional hours to the trip.

Afterwards, Dolly was so shook up she asked if I wouldn't mind laying down next to her and singing her to sleep, just as her sister had done when they were little'uns. I agreed as I knowed what it was like to feelin' all alone in the world, so I snuggled up next to her and sang a few verses of *Mary Blane*, though I could not do it much justice without Pa's banjo strumming to accompany me.

When I woke, she was gone. I looked everywhere, finally finding her in the small sleeping compartment I'd shared with Jasper. His case of wares was flung open, and from what I could count, eight or so empty bottles of "Thinking Tonic" were scattered about the floor. Dolly was deader than a dodger, but before she went, it looked as if she'd had a go with the Manipulator. Apparently, her womb had been a-wandering after all.

From the small sliver of light that poked out from under the curtain, I knew that dawn was not far off and I best skedaddle out of there lickity split. I grabbed the ruby brooch off the dressing table, deciding last minute to look in the place where every woman keeps her most cherished possession, her petticoat pocket. It was there that I found the letter from Horace, and a family photo folded into quarters with the names written on the back: Mother, Father, Eliza, and Dolly.

Pa would be proud that my painting skills would once again come in handy, and I quite liked the name Eliza. It would be a much pleasant change to being called *Girl*.

About the Author

Nikki Blakely lives in the San Francisco Bay Area and enjoys writing stories that evoke smiles, tears, laughter, the occasional eye roll, and sometimes even a scream. Her work has appeared in Black Cat Weekly, Short Edition, Uncharted, Sundial Magazine, Bright Flash Literary Review, Luna Station Quarterly, The Centifictionist, Writers Resist, Tall-Tale TV, The Lunatics Radio Hour, Cafe Lit, *and in the anthologies* Madame Gray's Boneyard of Blood *and* Dim and Flaring Lamps: A Historical Fiction Anthology of America.

You can read more of her work at www.nikkiblakely.com

Steal My Heart

by Bea Sage

Agent Raines hasn't liked this case from the beginning. She doesn't start hating it until she sees red cloth hanging from a gallery display case.

She'd taken point into the gallery, and immediately calls, "Stop!" Everyone does, in fits and starts; she hears one agent bump into another and mutter, "Sorry," because a real Interpol team is never going to function as smoothly as the ones on TV.

Jones pops up at her side in his usual jack-in-the-box appearance and asks, "Ma'am?"

It's testament to how concerned she is that she lets that lie, despite nigh-on two years of telling him not to call her that. "This isn't right. Keep everyone back."

She approaches the case, pulling gloves from her pocket, as he murmurs instructions behind her. The corner of the cloth has been tucked under the glass, leaving it hanging, moving minutely in the sterilised draught. The alarms linked to the case hadn't gone off, meaning Clara had already hijacked them, but Raines had clocked that nothing was gone as soon as she entered the room.

She checks again, turning slowly, matching walls and cases to the catalogue in her head. It's all there. Technically, Clara could have left a forgery in replacement—she's done it before—but, well. Raines doesn't like this job. And she really, really doesn't like the bandana she pulls from the case.

"Correll's," Jones says next to her. "That's not her usual M.O."

"Nope," she answers grimly. "Not her usual M.O. to not steal anything, either. Have we got the tapes?"

"As much as she left us."

"Pull them," Raines orders, and marches back out. Her team can collect the rest of the physical evidence. She has the important piece, in an evidence bag tucked into her chest pocket.

❖

Raines dreams in security footage.

The first time she ever saw Clara Correll, then an anonymous art thief caught in grainy black-and-white, handed over in a case file, cheekbones and half an eye.

Hours in a surveillance van watching an empty museum, only for the curator to call them in panicked recriminations the next morning; the almost-proud amusement Raines had barely repressed.

Raines' own first shots of her as she cased the Louvre, the image of bored French elite complete with red cloth tied jauntily around her neck. The ninety seconds they'd been in the same room before she slipped out from under them, where Raines had said, "Love the bandana," she'd complained, "It's a neckerchief. But thanks, Rosie," and Rosie Raines had been left to wonder how the hell Clara Correll knew her first name—and why she'd liked hearing her use it so much.

The shots of her, crystal-clear on the gallery's cameras the next day, still wearing the bandana-neckerchief.

A years-long chase across Europe, all with a bright smile and an accessory Raines had once said she liked, until she stopped thinking of her as Correll and spent her nights dreaming about being Rosie.

❖

"Ma'am!"

Raines jerks awake. There's a mug of shitty office coffee in front of her, hot, and Jones is sitting next to her at the briefing table. "Don't call me that," she mutters, and pulls a strand of hair from her mouth.

"Found anything?"

Clara, predictably, had looped the tapes before she ever appeared. Whoever took her—and Raines is sure, now, that she's been taken—wasn't as smart.

She turns the laptop she's been staring at to face Jones and points at the figure in the top right. "They're not supposed to be there. No logo on their uniform."

"Who's our mysterious stranger?"

"I'm running them."

The facial recognition program seems to like dramatic timing—that's the moment it chooses to chirp a notification.

Jones clicks on it before Raines can get there. "Geoffrey Smithson."

It takes Raines a moment, but, "Coventry. She took his Matisse."

"And he decided to go after her *himself*?"

Raines shrugs. "Rich idiots. Let's go."

✦

They track him to the warehouse district easily enough, and intercept him coming in.

On the cold ground surrounded by agents, with Raines looming over him, he starts to look like maybe the painting wasn't worth it.

"Where's Correll?" Raines demands.

The guy sneers at the gun in his face, because he's an idiot. Because he's an idiot, he also glances minutely at one of the warehouses behind Raines.

She's gone before anyone gets the chance to follow her.

◈

It's not the first time Raines has seen Clara face-to-face. That honor went to Barcelona, '09, either side of a Guárdia Urbana van. But it's the first time she's seen her vulnerable.

She's half-lying on the dirty ground, wrists tied roughly to a rusting pipe—until Rosie says, "Clara," when she looks up, green eyes still bright, and slips free.

"You got my message." Her voice is creaky, like she hasn't had water since yesterday afternoon, and there's a bruise spreading over her cheek and something that looks like a taser burn on bare skin under her ripped sleeves.

Rosie drops to the ground, holstering her gun and reaching out, like she can do anything to help.

Maybe she can, because Clara reaches back, keeps reaching, pulling Rosie down until their lips meet.

Now this—this is a first. Clara's touch gentle on her neck, the knotted silk of her hair through Rosie's fingers, lips cracked and dry but still soft, Rosie's pulse bounding under Clara's hand as her body processes what her brain can't.

Clara pulls back first; Rosie couldn't have. They stare at each other for seconds or hours, Clara's eyes moving from uncertain and a little scared through a brief flash of relief into horrendous smugness.

"Are you going to arrest me now?" she murmurs.

"Did you steal anything?" Rosie asks, knowing full well the answer.

"No," Clara answers, almost pouting.

"Nothing I can hold you on, then." It's a blatant lie; she still drugged a security guard and hacked into the system, not to mention a whole host of past thefts Interpol holds a tenuous but nonetheless existent string of evidence on. More damning than the lie is that when Clara smiles, slow and dimpled and self-satisfied in the knowledge that Raines is letting her go, Rosie is pretty sure she can live with it.

Silently, she hands over the bandana that's lived in her inside pocket since the gallery, and helps Clara to her feet.

"Go," is the only word uttered between them; Clara doesn't even obey it, twirling at the last second to press close, dropping her hand to Rosie's chest and her lips to Rosie's cheek before she flees.

❖

Raines waits until she's sitting alone in the front seat of a company car to check her chest pocket. She pulls out a red bandana, folded into a neat square.

With something prickling and burning behind her eyes, she shakes it out. A small square of white paper flutters down into her lap.

Thank you, it reads in neat black ink, then, underneath, *see you in Munich* with a heart outlined after it.

Rosie laughs over tears, and reaches for her phone. "Jones. Pack for Germany."

About the Author

Bea Sage is actually three writers stacked on top of each other wearing a trench coat. Together, they've gotten some of those words into publications including 72 Hours of Insanity: Writer's Games *volumes 7, 9, 10, and 13,* Red Penguin's A Heart Full of Love, Kapow!, *Murderous Ink Press's* The Cosy Nostra, *Romance Writers of Australia's* Diversions—Lights, *and online at* Defenestration *and* Bullshit Lit. *They've also placed in the Writer's Workout Writer's Games for five consecutive years.*

THE SCARF THIEF

BY HEATHER SANTO

A troll stole Frankie's scarf.

She was halfway up an eastern white pine tree when it happened, even though her older brother Jack strictly forbade climbing. Frankie couldn't help herself. She was drawn to trees, especially the tall pine behind their RV. From the high vantage point, she could see for miles in every direction.

Below, Jack sat at the picnic table, studying an atlas and several local maps. Bella, their shih tzu, snoozed at his feet.

Clothes flapped on a line strung between two metal poles on their rental lot. That morning, they'd washed a few loads at the town laundromat and brought everything back to hang dry. The poles, now mostly rusted, looked like they had once been painted white.

Their father's "adventure scarf," as Frankie referred to it, a desert tan shemagh, was pinned to the section of line furthest from Jack. Frankie wore it every day, even on August scorchers like this one, but after her last trip up the pine, she'd been covered in sap.

Jack had insisted she wash the scarf.

There was rustling inside the tree line. Frankie glanced down and wasn't sure what she was seeing. Some kind of animal, maybe? A weird breed of dog or possibly a mangy bear. It scampered across the lot and yanked the scarf off the clothesline.

Her brother, intently focused on the maps, didn't notice.

Bella, however, did.

The dog jolted awake and immediately began barking. The short gray figure paused, turning around to stare at the shih tzu. Frankie realized it *definitely* wasn't a dog. The creature stood upright, walking on two stumpy legs. Its arms were so long they almost dragged on the ground. One meaty hand still clutched the scarf.

Most ten-year-olds would have been paralyzed with fear. Not Frankie. Excitement pumped wildly through her system.

"Bella, shut *up*," Jack said. Not looking up, he nudged the shih tzu gently with the toe of his sneaker.

Bella, however, did *not* shut up.

The creature tilted its head, one ear inclined toward her brother and dog.

"What has gotten into you?" Jack demanded as Bella hopped around the table, yapping incessantly.

Then, her brother's head snapped up.

"Frankie, where are you?"

She didn't respond. The creature was directly underneath the pine. It plodded about and raised its bulbous nose, nostrils flaring.

Could it *smell* her?

"Frankie!"

She shifted on the branch and the creature jerked its head in her direction.

"What *are* you?" she whispered.

And then, as suddenly as it had appeared, the creature was gone.

"If you're in that tree again, Frankie, I'm going to flip out!"

She slid down the trunk, snapping branches and scraping her left forearm. Needles clung to her dark hair, and her feet stung when they hit the ground.

Jack appeared in front of her, hands on his hips.

"I knew it."

Frankie wiped sticky sap on her shorts.

"Did you see it?"

Her brother's forehead creased in confusion.

166

"See what?"

"I don't know." Frankie knelt to pet Bella, who pawed at her legs. "Some kind of creature. It stole my scarf off the clothesline."

Jack glanced over his shoulder and sighed deeply. When he looked back, he wore the worried expression of someone much older than eighteen.

"Look, I don't know what you saw, or where the scarf went, but that doesn't change the fact that you went climbing again. I'm doing the best I can under the circumstances. Dad left us with nothing but that Winnebago, some cash, and a mysterious scroll." He pounded one fist into his other open palm. "I'm trying to figure out where the scroll leads, where Dad *wanted* to go, but I can't do that if you keep running off and climbing trees. What if you fall and get hurt? How am I going to explain our situation to some doctor at the emergency room?"

She cast her eyes at the ground. "I'm not going to fall."

"You don't know that," he said.

"I do! Just like I saw something steal the scarf. Bella saw it too, that's why she was barking."

Jack scooped up the shih tzu.

"No, she knew you were in the tree. That's why she was barking."

Frankie stomped her foot.

"You never believe me."

"I'm doing the best I can. Really, I am."

Tears leaked from Frankie's eyes. "I am too."

Her brother grabbed her hand, gave it a reassuring squeeze.

"I know," he said. "Do you want to go into town with me? My eyes could use a break from these maps, and we need some groceries."

Frankie hesitated. "Do I have to?"

Her brother set down the squirming dog.

"No," he replied. "As long as you promise not to climb any more trees."

"Can I go look for the scarf?"

He considered this.

"Okay, but stay in the Confluence RV Park. No wandering off. I mean it." He started to turn and stopped. "And take Bella with you."

❖

"Don't tell Jack we left the RV park," Frankie said to the shih tzu. She clipped the leash onto the dog's harness and set out for the woods. There was an overgrown trail west of the pine tree, and Frankie had a hunch the scarf thief had gone that way.

Unlike her own life, everything in the forest felt balanced. Sun streamed through the leaf canopy and warblers sang as Frankie and Bella picked their way through the tangled summer overgrowth.

"There it is." She spotted the trail and led the dog farther down, toward the river. They walked parallel to the railroad tracks, along the snaking tributary that would eventually empty into Yough Lake.

"It couldn't have gotten far. Not on those stumpy legs."

Bella barked in agreement, her own short legs working furiously to keep up.

"Stop," Frankie instructed. Just ahead, she spotted the gray creature, lumbering down the trail about a hundred yards ahead. "I *knew* it."

They followed, keeping as much distance as possible between themselves and the scarf thief without losing sight of it. Soon, Frankie heard vehicle traffic where the Route 281 overpass crossed River Road.

"The bridge, *of course*," she said. It was all making sense now. Sweat trickled down her back and the scrape on her arm burned. Bella paused to mark an oak tree.

"It's a troll. Must be," she decided. She watched the creature break away from the trail and scale the hillside leading up to the bridge.

"C'mon, let's go get my scarf."

⬥

Truck fumes and damp earth filled Frankie's nostrils. And something almost spicy. Like cinnamon, but not quite. Bella whimpered as she dragged the dog up the hill and underneath the bridge. It was dark, but enough daylight filtered through that she could make out the concrete abutment against this side of the river. The ground leveled off, soft but not too muddy, under her shoes.

A circular shape, roughly the size of a large tractor tire on its side, caught her eye. The closer she got, she realized it was a nest, constructed from branches and other haphazard items.

The troll, if that's what it was, was nowhere in sight.

Frankie approached the nest. Plastic soda bottles stuck out of the structure here and there, as well as pieces of random clothing. A T-shirt, blue swim trunks, so many socks. At its edge, which came up to her hip, Frankie leaned over and peered inside.

The bottom of the nest was covered with coins, fishing lures, and bottle caps.

"What in the world?" Frankie wondered, just as she spotted her scarf. It was woven into the opposite side of the nest. Determined, she marched over and started pulling it loose.

Bella growled, deep and low.

"Shhhh," Frankie said. "Just another minute and we can get out of here." But before she could free her scarf, the troll trudged around the other side of the abutment, crunching a mouthful of dandelions.

It stopped short, one yellow flower sticking out of its mouth like a clay pipe.

They stared at each other for several moments.

Finally, Frankie said, "Hello."

The troll's mouth fell open and the dandelion rolled out.

"You can see me?" it said in a gravelly voice.

"Y-yes." Frankie stood, balling the scarf up in her hands. She was a full head taller than the creature, but it had sharp, pointed teeth and claw-like nails.

"How did you find me?"

"I followed you." She raised her chin and lifted the scarf. "You stole this, and I came to get it back."

The troll scratched its bald head. It wore a dirty white tank top that hung just above its knobby knees. The shade of its skin blended almost perfectly with the concrete pilings. Frankie couldn't discern a gender, but something about the creature suggested it was male.

"I... thought it smelled familiar," the troll said, nostrils flaring. It regarded her with oily black eyes. "Something about you smells familiar too."

"Well, I've never met a troll before. I thought they were made up, like unicorns and dragons."

The troll scoffed. "Made up? Unicorns certainly. But not trolls." It paused. "Or dragons."

The shih tzu inched forward and sniffed the troll's feet.

"Who do we have here?" it asked.

"This is Bella," she replied. "I'm Frankie."

"Frankie?" The troll scratched its head again. "That's a funny name for a human girl."

It was her turn to be offended. "It's short for Frances, after my grandmother."

Those oily black eyes widened. "Would that be your father's mother?"

"How do you know that?"

The troll ignored her question.

"I'm Mudvak," it said, and extended a hand. "Sorry about the scarf."

She shook hands with the troll. "Is that a common troll name?"

"In my world, I come from the mud lands. Hence, Mudvak."

It stooped down and gave Bella's ears a good rub. She immediately rolled over and showed her belly. A good sign, Frankie thought. She could usually trust the dog's judgment when it came to people.

Hopefully that extended to trolls.

"What are you doing here?" she asked.

"I'm a guard troll. I'm here... guarding something."

"Okay," Frankie said. "And people can't usually see you?"

"Only *certain* people can see me."

She gestured at the nest.

"If you've never seen a troll before, safe to say you've never seen a troll nest before, either."

"What's it for?" she asked.

"Sleeping mostly."

Frankie nodded, as if that made total sense.

"My brother didn't believe me," she said. "When I told him I saw you."

"You tell anyone else? Like your mom or dad?"

"My mom died when I was little. And my dad—" she clutched the scarf to her chest "—he was on an airplane that crashed a few months ago. No survivors." She took a deep breath. "It's just me and Jack now."

The dog barked.

"Oh, and Bella."

"Staying at the RV park?" the troll asked.

"Yeah, my dad left behind this scroll, and my brother thinks it's a clue to some big treasure. There's a map of this area on the scroll, but before—" Frankie waved her arms at the bridge "—all this was here."

Mudvak grabbed her wrist. She cried out in surprise more than pain, although it was her injured arm.

"I'm sorry." The troll released her, scraped mud from beside its nest, and rubbed it on her scrape. "That should help."

"Thank you," Frankie said. The burning sensation was already dissipating.

"Now," Mudvak said, "I'd like to see this scroll."

✦

"You brought home a troll!"

Jack hurried around the 1966 Brave Winnebago, pulling window curtains shut. He'd been putting away canned goods when they arrived. "It's bad enough we're surrounded by nosy, retired couples with nothing better to do than ask *very* detailed questions that I have to feed lies to, and then you waltz up with an actual troll!"

Frankie sat at the U-shaped dinette with the troll on one side of her, shih tzu on the other. "I told you I saw something this morning. Well, this is Mudvak."

"Pleasure to meet you." The troll extended a hand.

Her brother stopped, looked at Mudvak's hand, and started laughing uncontrollably.

"I'm dreaming." Her brother scrubbed his hands over his face. "I must be. Either that or I'm having some kind of psychotic break. There is no way a troll, a *polite* troll I might add, is sitting at the table."

"So, you can see him too?" Frankie looked at Mudvak. "What does that mean, exactly? You said earlier only certain people can see you."

"We'll get into that later. First, I'd like to see the scroll."

Jack's eyes widened. "You told him about the scroll!"

She raised her arms. "I didn't see what it could hurt."

"Didn't see what it could hurt?" His voice raised several octaves. "Only *everything*, Frankie!"

Bella pawed at her. She gave the dog a milk bone from a nearby tin.

"He's a guard troll, Jack. Maybe he can help."

Mudvak reached for the tin, popped a bone into his mouth. "Mmm, tasty. Now, about that scroll. May I?" The troll pointed to a roll of paper towels.

Her brother threw his hands in the air.

"Be my guest."

"Thank you." Mudvak turned to Frankie. "Do you have a pen?"

"There's one attached to a magnet of the fridge. Jack, will you grab it?"

Her brother's face was beet red. Without a word, he retrieved the pen and handed it to his sister.

She passed it to the troll, and watched as he stretched out a length of paper towel and began to draw. Frankie shifted, sitting up on her knees to see better.

"What are you drawing?" she asked.

"A map," Jack answered, tugging thoughtfully on his spiky black hair. "And not just any map." He went to the front of the RV, unlocked the glove box, and removed the scroll.

When Mudvak finished, her brother opened the scroll next to the paper towel, placing a can of baked beans on either end to keep it from rolling back up. Everyone around the table, Bella included, leaned in.

"They're identical," Jack breathed. "But I don't understand. How?"

"Easy," the troll replied. He tapped the scroll. "I made the original."

❖

An hour later, they gathered back at the dinette. Jack had told everyone he needed some time to think, and while he thought, he prepared a boxed macaroni and cheese dinner, served with a side of baked beans.

"What happened to the scroll? Did you lose it?" Frankie pushed noodles around her plate. She was too excited to eat.

"No, someone stole it from me. Someone I considered a dear friend and ally." Mudvak slurped beans.

"Who?" her brother asked.

The troll pointed at Jack with his plastic fork.

"Your father. So technically, I was justified in stealing the scarf."

"That doesn't make sense. Our father is, I mean *was,*" Jack corrected, "an adventurer. A great treasure hunter, but he didn't know any trolls."

"None that he told you about," Mudvak corrected.

Jack fell silent.

"Does that have something to do with why we can see you?" Frankie asked.

"Smart girl." The troll licked his plate. "This is delicious, by the way. Yes, you can see me because your father was originally from my world."

"Wait, you mean he's not human?" Jack looked at his sister. "That we're technically not human?"

"I wouldn't say that." Mudvak was thoughtful. "More like *magical* humans."

Frankie pounded her fist on the table. "I knew it!"

❖

"You did good," the troll said. Brother, sister, and dog all followed him in the growing twilight, down the street toward an old junkyard. "Got within spitting distance of what you were looking for."

"The Confluence was the biggest clue, and once I realized this map predated the manmade lake, I followed the Allegheny Mountain range, and it led me here." Jack kicked a rock on the road. "But I've been through the junkyard a dozen times. Didn't find anything. I figured I was reading the scroll wrong."

They reached a chain link fence. Jack held back a section he'd sliced with bolt cutters.

"Like I said," Mudvak replied as he slipped through the fence, "spitting distance."

◆

Frankie carried Bella through the maze of old cars, boats, home appliances, and piles of rusted metal. "Is whatever you guard here?" she asked.

"Yes, it is. After your father stole the scroll, I was sentenced to stand watch and make sure no human—no non-magical humans, that is—discovered it."

Mudvak stopped and, with a flourish, indicated a 1966 mint green Volkswagen Beetle among the towering scrap.

"This isn't treasure," Jack said. "It's just an old car."

"That, my dear boy, is where you are wrong. The map doesn't lead to *treasure*." With one meaty hand, the troll slapped the trunk of the Beetle. It flew open, and amber light poured out.

That spicy, not-quite-cinnamon scent hit Frankie like a wall.

"It's a portal," Mudvak said. "To my world."

She approached the open trunk. So many trees, she thought, in dazzling jewel tones. Twin rivers. And was that a *dragon* swooping across the brilliant sky?

Jack was at her side.

"It's beautiful," he said.

"Magical," Frankie added.

Bella, squirming in her arms, barked in agreement.

"What do you say," Mudvak said. "Ready to go home?"

She clutched the scarf around her neck, glanced at Jack, and turned to face the troll.

"Yes," she said. "Let's go."

About the Author

Heather Santo is a procurement category manager living in Pittsburgh, PA, with her husband and two children. In addition to writing, her interests include photography, travel, and collecting skeleton keys.

Her educational background is in biochemistry, forensic science, and law.

In the past two years, she's had short stories published by Flash Point SF, NewMyths Magazine, *and* Amazing Stories.

You can follow her on Instagram and X @Heather52384.

THE FINAL PORTRAIT

BY S.L. KRETSCHMER

The bus engine rumbles as my fellow tour group members board. Twenty-four relative strangers making the pilgrimage, I think, each for their own reasons. I am sure many are history buffs, like me, tingling with the anticipation of seeing with our own eyes what, up to now, has only been words and pictures. A small red-headed woman sitting next to me sniffs the air in my direction.

"Ooh. You smell pretty," she says. "Is that Chanel Mademoiselle?"

I smile, opening my backpack and holding it toward her.

"No," I say, a small chuckle escaping at the thought of a poor, just finished university student affording Chanel. "It's Dove."

She looks in my bag at the deodorant stick.

"Well, to be sure, my deodorant never smelled as good on me. And Dove. Quite contrary to today, isn't it?" she chirrups in a lilting Irish accent.

I'm not following her. It must show on my face.

"Dove. Peace?"

I nod slowly and take a deep breath, looking out the window. It may be a long ride.

❖

It takes three hours to get from Lille to Thiepval. Our tour guide, a jovial Brit named Brett, stands at the front of the bus, bouncing with energy, and regales us with stories of the 1916 battlefields. The roads are full of ruts, and he struggles to maintain his balance.

"Who among you has a family connection to the Somme?" he asks.

The redhead, whom I now know has the name Joyce, raises her hand. Our initial first contact has mellowed into a mutual respect for solitude and reflection. She looks at me and smiles.

"My great-great-uncle fought with the Irish Guard."

I want to raise mine, but instead fold my hands and place them in my lap. For the last three years, my life has revolved around the war artist William Orpen. He feels like family to me. Two weeks ago, I submitted my thesis on his depictions of the Somme. And now I'm finally here.

My heart pounds as I leave the bus. I try to picture the landscape Orpen saw, but the monument makes it nearly impossible to do so. The rural scene is dominated by interlocking stone arches, the central arch soaring one hundred and forty feet above the fields and the Thiepval Wood surrounding it. I hear Brett explain that more than 72,000 names are engraved on the memorial, but I'm not really listening. I'm here for the wood, not the monument.

While the others turn left, I head right, following a narrow gravel path toward the forest. A tremor runs down my back. It is easier to imagine the devastation Orpen had seen here: a land devoid of any living thing, pitted with craters and littered with broken bodies. The woods themselves are a cemetery for those who died here, their bodies forever a part of the fertile soil, the trees their headstones, the rough bark their epitaph. I search for remnants of a walkway, a crater. I will myself to find the place, making promises and pacts to whomever or whatever can help me. And finally, I do.

Opening my backpack, I take out a print of Orpen's painting, my sketch pad, and pencils. The painting depicts the body of a soldier lying on the broken timber of a makeshift walkway. One arm is thrown above his head—his eyes stare at the sky, unseeing. Dark hair frames his face; blood pools beneath him. He lies beside a flooded shell hole. I want to draw the scene as it is today. To put closure to my years of study. Suddenly an image comes to mind which has a realism that scares me. I close my eyes tightly, sensing a change in the wood, a darkness that wasn't there before. I shudder involuntarily and recall that Orpen felt these woods haunted. He'd claimed to have been attacked while painting, although his was the only heart beating.

❖

The temperature drops and a whisper surrounds me.

"Why've ye got me painting?"

Startled, I open my eyes, but I'm alone. The voice comes to me again, but louder, more malevolent.

"I said, why've ye got me painting? Are ye his blood?"

I hesitate, my heart in my throat. I say the words out loud without realizing I'm saying them.

"Whose blood?" I whisper.

My stomach convulses as the stench of rotting flesh permeates my nostrils. A blast of cold air whips around me and the picture is wrenched from my hand. I watch as it levitates in mid-air.

"I naw wanna be remembered like this," the voice booms in my ear. "What if Mam or Da saw it? Or my Creena?"

The faintest shadow of a man begins to form in a gray mist that has rolled from the earth, emerging like a plume of smoke. A soldier, no more than eighteen or nineteen, stands a few feet away, his dark hair slick with blood, khaki uniform ripped and stained. His fingers grip Orpen's painting.

"I tried to stop him, told him to feck off. I naw wanted this! This isn't me! A manky body lying next to putrid water. Me death was only a wee part of me! He stole me life by showing me death. He should've painted me like the buck I was!"

His anguished wail tore at my heart.

"Please," I say shakily, "he didn't mean any harm. The man who painted this was deeply affected, broken even, from all he had seen. Visions of death clouded his sleep. What can I do to help you? How can I give you peace?"

The apparition points to my sketch pad.

"Will ye draw me as I was?"

Nodding, I pick up my pad and begin to sketch the soldier. I ignore the weeping crater that was his skull. I erase the bloody shrapnel that peppers his body. I work like a woman possessed. Finally, I hold up his portrait. A proud young man, black hair slicked back, uniform pristine.

"Thank ye," he whispers. The Orpen print flutters down to the verdant soil as his shadow dissipates into the woods.

❖

I'm trembling when I reboard the bus, physically and mentally exhausted. I sit down and look at the portrait I've drawn, doubting all that just happened. Joyce eases herself into the seat next to me. I hear her gasp; trembling fingers reach down and touch my drawing. I look up at Joyce, her face devoid of color.

"My god! Where did you find that? That's my Uncle Jimmy!"

I look at her, confused.

"Here, I'll show you," she whispers shakily.

With fumbling hands, she retrieves a faded photo of her great-great-uncle from a worn leather purse. A handsome young man, black hair slicked back, uniform pristine, a look of pride on his face. We look at each other, our eyes wet with tears. She seems to need no explanation, and I offer her none.

"Here," I say, placing the portrait in her lap. "Take it. Take Jimmy home."

About the Author

S.L. Kretschmer is a South Australian writer based in the Barossa Valley. She holds a BA in Creative Writing and postgraduate qualifications in Museum Studies, reflecting her love for both storytelling and history. Her short fiction has appeared in anthologies and journals including Until Dawn, Inscribe Literary, Beyond Words, *and* Bluing the Blade. *Her stories for children have been published in* The School Magazine *(NSW Department of Education). When not writing, she enjoys connecting with a very special global community of writers, Zumba, wandering local cemeteries, and sending her adult children random thoughts.*

CAMOUFLAGE

BY LISA FOX

So, this is what it's like to breathe in Hell.

The arid, gritty air grates my teeth, my tongue, my throat; it's sandpaper to my lungs as I suck in deep gulps, heaving one breath after another. My once-black MGM Grand T-shirt clings with desert sweat. Dusty hues of the Grand Canyon paint me with the guilt of my crime. I lean into the canyon wall, a salamander channeling its camouflage as angry searchers scan the vast expanse, hoping for the slightest glimpse of me under the hundred-and-four-degree spotlight that is the sun.

It's usually an easy scam, only five steps to victory.

One: Dress like a tourist. Vegas T-shirt, Jansport backpack, New York Yankees cap, Nikes with worn soles, scratched wire-framed Ray-Bans.

Two: Wander into the crowd. Target the most enthusiastic site oglers—those who lack the proper degree of *situational awareness*.

Three: Lift their wares, swift as the wind.

Four: Disappear into the crowd, meandering from tour group to tour group until I've reached the parking lot.

Five: Escape. Comfortable in the driver's seat of... my black Ford Escape.

Fitting, isn't it?

I'm halfway back to Vegas before they know what's missing.

In six months' time, I've amassed thirty thousand dollars in cash, fifteen iPhones, two gold teeth, and a diamond engagement ring.

It's an easy living, but not today—thanks to the small, pale, and exceptionally bored blond-haired boy playing *Pokémon Go* on a cell phone.

Who knew that was still a thing?

With the virtual *Pokémon* character taunting him through the tiny screen, the kid caught me in the ultimate photo bomb—just as I stashed a woman's small, red canvas duffle bag into my backpack.

"Mom. Mom!" The boy tugged at his mother's meaty arm. She swatted him back as she squinted through the binoculars glued to her eyeballs.

"MOM! She STOLE that lady's bag!"

I felt the whiplash of eighteen tourist heads snap in my direction, their quick, accusing eyes lancing into me. A middle-aged woman screamed with the realization that her satchel had vanished—*poof!*—like in a Copperfield show.

"Thief!"

I ran without thought, without direction—adrenaline overtaking my body and my brain. I dashed through the crowd, a clay dust cloud in my wake. I ran past the Desert View Watchtower of Grand Canyon National Park, past the native Hopis selling their weavings—their deep, knowing eyes following as I fled down the steep slope to a narrow ridge overlooking the canyon bed.

Angry voices echo as I quickly unzip the screaming-woman's bag. Sherrie Miller, 43, from Milwaukee, Wisconsin, has furnished me with a stick of Cinnamon Red Cover Girl lipstick, a hair scrunchie decorated with miniature Elvises (or is it Elvis-ae?), a yellow Bic lighter, and half a pack of Marlboros. Digging deeper, I find a white handkerchief, one hundred and sixty-three dollars in cash, men's horn-rimmed eyeglasses, and a red T-shirt with "Keep Calm and Play Slots" emblazoned on the front. Anchoring the bottom of the bag is a black Totes travel-sized umbrella.

Nothing in this sack warrants a mug shot.

The distance between me and my Ford is too vast for a ready getaway. By now, I'm certain security is swarming, guarding each exit, as the hapless victim files her report. My only options: amble down the steep decline and hide at the bed of the canyon, prey in wait; or turn back, ascend the dusty gradient, and find a way out.

I peer over the precipice separating me from the canyon floor. Tumbleweed drifts over the jagged slope. Somewhere in the distance, the distinctive clatter of a rattlesnake melds with the heat in a veritable sizzle. To dive deep into the desert haze and wallow in the belly of hell, indefinitely, without water or shelter save for the shade of a Totes umbrella would precipitate certain suicide.

I decide to turn back.

But first, I peel away my sweat-soaked T-shirt. I toss my Yankees cap and Ray-Bans aside and use the victim's handkerchief to wipe the grime from my body. I turn the red "Keep Calm" T-shirt inside out and pull it over my head, appreciating its clean coolness. I pull my long hair up in an Elvis-secured bun. I don the horn-rimmed glasses. They bear thin, slightly tinted lenses that thicken the canyon haze.

It will do.

I loop the umbrella cord around my wrist, pack the cash, Marlboros, and lighter in my back pocket, and carefully engage in my ascent.

I still hear the woman shrilling loudly in the distance and the murmurs of officers reassuring her that the *perpetrator* (me) will be found and her *valuables* (questionable) retrieved.

I tread one foot at a time, ensuring my steps do not prompt a rockslide or worse—a fall into the canyon.

I reach the top of the ridge, the Watchtower to my right. Groups of tourists mill about, crowding around an elderly craftsman as he weaves an intricate tapestry. Save for the woman's distant cacophony, it's quiet here. No one notices me materialize.

I open the umbrella, cloaking myself in its invisibility like some deranged Harry Potter.

Unsmiling officers—tall and rigid—block the path to the parking lot. They're prickly as cactus. A pudgy, red-faced cop hovers over the blond-haired child as he shares the cell phone screen implicating me and the precious Pokémon.

Turning away, I crouch under the sanctuary of my umbrella.

A chopper whirs in the distance. I find my oasis on a splintered wooden sign, painted in crimson: *Helicopter Tours Over the Grand Canyon: One-Way to Las Vegas.*

I approach the ticket counter. The portly, disheveled agent extends a filthy hand to accept my stolen one hundred and fifty dollars and absently slides me a crisp ticket. His eyes never leave his cell phone screen.

I release a Marlboro from its sheath, light it, and inhale.

So this is what it's like to breathe in Hell. Sometimes, it's just too easy.

About the Author

Lisa Fox loves to ask questions. By day, she's a pharmaceutical market researcher. By night, she channels that same inquisitive spirit into writing short fiction, building worlds and characters that explore the meaning of life, the universe, and everything in between. She survives, and sometimes thrives, in the chaos of suburban New Jersey with her husband, two sons, and quirky Double-Doodle dog. Lisa is an award-winning author of three short story collections: A Treatise on Martian Chiropractic Manipulation and Other Satirical Tales, Core Truths, *and* Passageways: Short Speculative Fiction.

Website: lisafoxiswriting.com Twitter/X: @iamlisafox10800 Facebook: lisafoxiswriting

MY LEGACY

BY ANDREA GOYAN

What drives me? I bet you wish I'd say you, but my urges began long before I got you, baby. However, you are my legacy, and I will teach you everything.

Here are my secrets.

1) Passion.

I love moving into a new house—the excitement and possibilities, the grift called upward mobility. An opportunity to assimilate remains more tantalizing than any new-car smell. No one suspects my humble beginnings, and those roots never hold me down. In fact, the specter of the smelly, orange shag carpeting in my childhood's one-bedroom apartment motivates me.

Mine is a long game called the American Dream. I am its exemplar and avatar. You will follow in my footsteps.

2) Armor.

Don't ever let anyone possess your heart.

People have called me many things like cheater, thief, liar, bitch, but their admonishments come too late. They say it to my dust, to the back of my car as I drive away, to the moving van carrying away their prized possessions. They mistook my false kindness for real friendship.

Idiots. Or, more precisely, marks.

But before I burrow beneath their skin and into their secrets, I need to gain their...

3) Trust.

- Bake cookies. The best way to integrate yourself and make friends is to bring offerings. When they ask, "What's the occasion?" say you wanted to introduce yourself to your new neighbors. Say you're celebrating the beautiful neighborhood. Tell them their roses make you smile every day, so you wanted to return the gift. Make up anything that sounds neighborly.

- Wake up early on alternate street parking days so you can be the one to remind anyone who's forgotten to move their car. You are a do-goodie-two-shoes!

- Make friends. Get a dog or, better yet, a puppy. Baby animals are magnets. Walk the puppy two or three times a day. You'll meet all kinds of neighbors. And their kids will flock to you. Kiddos have loose lips. They're unknowing assets, and precious bits of intel can spill from the mouths of babes. Ask things like: Do you have a dog? What kind? Learn if they leave it outside or in when they're away from home.

- Summer barbeques in your fabulous backyard. Need I say more?

- Befriend the neighborhood gossip.

- Start a book club.

4) Payout.

I hate when people say what I do isn't a job. I work hard. My profession demands 24/7 vigilance. I am always alert, looking for fissures in the neighborhood filament. Ways to use my lovely neighbors' avarice against them.

Did Bobby's father come home with some hot young thing who wasn't his wife, Jan, while Jan was at her Pilates class?

Why are cars coming and going to Tucker's house at all hours?
Drug deals?

Oh, Susan, you didn't pull permits for that kitchen remodel...

5) Love.

I told myself don't do it, remember rule two, but when I saw you in your stroller... Don't cry, baby. That other woman didn't deserve you. Together, our future is bright. You are my legacy.

About the Author

Andrea Goyan is an award-winning writer, playwright, and poet. Her novel The Catalyst *is serialized at Metastellar.com. She's part of a women's poetry collective. Their collection,* An Illegal Feast, *was published in 2025. In her spare time, she paints, walks her dogs, and co-hosts MetaStellar's* Long-Lost Friends and Storytime.

More of her work is available on her website andreagoyan.com. Follow her on Facebook @Andrea Goyan Storyteller, Bluesky@AndreaGoyan, and Substack Mutations & Manuscripts | Substack

WHEN MEN WEAR PINK

BY LESLIE MUZINGO

The "Biloxi Three," as they called themselves, sat on the white sand discussing their next caper. Their leader, Mickey, devoured shrimp while he talked.

"Inside, cameras are everywhere. But during the Blessing of the Fleet, Pharaoh's Casino is gonna move its slot machines onto the beach and—"

"Why?" asked Bubba as he peeled Mickey's shrimp.

"Why, what?" Mickey demanded.

"Why are they moving their slot machines onto the beach?"

"Damn it, Bubba, who frigging cares? Probably they'll get lots of business during the Blessing, what with so many Catholics on the beach. And don't ask me how they hook up the electricity cuz I don't know."

"Don't be nasty to Bubba," said Claude. "He ain't bright."

"That's right. I ain't bright," added Bubba, popping a shrimp in his mouth when Mickey wasn't looking.

Mickey slapped his forehead. "Just listen, okay? They're moving the slot machines onto the beach. Claude, that makes it easier for you to rig one to win because there won't be any cameras."

Claude looked skeptical. "But I gotta be under it for a couple of minutes. Someone is still sure to notice. You got a cover-up plan for me, boss?"

Mickey grinned. "Ya'll come to my house at 7 a.m. Saturday. Claude, bring your tools. Bubba, you be clean! I'll give you the details then."

Claude and Bubba arrived only fifteen minutes late on Saturday. Claude brought his tools. Bubba brought a dirty face.

"I said come clean!" Micky said.

"I am clean. This is just breakfast." Bubba pointed to his cheek.

While he scrubbed Bubba's face, Mickey explained the plan. "You know those girls, the Biloxi Belles? They'll be at the Blessing of the Fleet today. We're gonna make Bubba up like one of 'em with a pink hoop skirt, wig, and makeup."

"What! No, not me!" Bubba cried from under the wash rag.

Mickey continued, "Claude, you'll be under Bubba's skirt on your knees. I got ya some knee pads. Bubba will stand by a vacant slot machine. There's a slit in the dress for you to pull apart and work on the machine. When it's ready, I play it and we get a big win!"

"I like it," Claude said with a nod.

"I don't," Bubba said, shaking his head.

"Two against one, so it's a go. Let's get Bubba dressed up. The Blessing starts in a few hours," Mickey said.

"I don't like this, I don't like this," Bubba repeated as they made up his face.

"Shut up, you'll be gorgeous."

"Should he wear blue eyeshadow?" Claude asked.

Mickey nodded. "Absolutely. With those pink cheeks, he'll be the prettiest belle on the beach!"

"His eyelashes are so long!" Claude said as he applied the eyeshadow.

"He'll look like a little doll!" Mickey grinned. "Who knew he could clean up so good?"

Once they had Bubba dressed, they all took a moment to admire their creation. Claude donned the kneepads and dove under Bubba's dress. The two practiced walking together. The first time was a catastrophe. Bubba tripped over Claude's feet, and the hoop skirt upended with both fellas underneath it. It took a couple more mishaps for them to get the right speed and rhythm.

"Great!" Mickey said. "Let's go make some money!"

The beach was crowded, but Mickey played interference to get Bubba through. Claude crawled under Bubba's skirt before the crowd thinned out. Before long, they made their way to where the slot machines were set up.

"Wow," Mickey said. "All these slot machines overlook the sea. I wish I had a camera."

"I wish I could see it," Claude grumbled from under Bubba's skirt.

"They're also setting up a buffet... look at that shrimp..." Mickey muttered.

"Mickey, can we get started? I feel stupid standing here dressed like a girl," Bubba said.

"Sure, Bubba. Remember, rap your fan three times into your palm when Claude is done."

While Claude worked, Bubba played with his fan. He decided that being a girl wasn't all that bad. He'd always liked pink, but guys didn't wear it. Not any guys he knew, anyway.

Bubba noticed a handsome man coming his way. He opened his fan and put it up to his face to cover his smile.

Meanwhile, Mickey evaluated the buffet. There were fried shrimp, sauteed shrimp, and his favorite, boiled shrimp. Best yet, the boiled shrimp were already peeled! But those damn tourists were sure to eat them all once the Blessing was over. He couldn't let that happen. No, he just couldn't.

Claude knew he could make this work because Pharaoh used old slot machines. The new ones were computerized, but these old ones could be adjusted by changing the reel strips and the sensing disks. He quickly made the adjustments. He wanted to tell Bubba it was time to signal Mickey, but for some time he'd been hearing a conversation where some guy was telling Bubba that he "was ever so bee-u-ti-ful" and "had the blewist eyes." When the fella asked Bubba for a "teeny-weeny kiss," Claude figured he better help his friend out and save him from this guy who was obviously a New Orleans cad, so he pulled a hair on Bubba's thigh. He heard Bubba cry out, and after a "sees ya later," the male voice was gone.

Focused once more, Bubba rapped his fan three times, but Mickey was nowhere to be seen. Bubba rapped three more times. He was about to rap again when a wrinkled Vietnamese woman approached him.

"Me play machine."

"This is mine," Bubba said, rapping his fan three times in his palm

"You not play. Me play machine," the woman said.

"Claude, gimme a quarter!" Bubba hissed.

"Man-ee-ger!"

Bubba and Claude retreated to the bells and whistles of a slot machine hitting it big. They found Mickey eating his fifth plate of shrimp.

"We got nothing for our trouble?" Mickey asked with his mouth full.

"I wouldn't say that." Bubba giggled as he fluttered his fan before his eyes. "Pretty me got a hot date for Thursday night. I'll need the two of you to do my makeup."

About the Author

Leslie's writing focuses mostly on character. She won first place four times in the Two Sisters' Writing and Publishing Anthologies I & II *and was a finalist in the* Scribes Valley Contest *three years running, earning a spot in their anthologies. Her work is listed on Goodreads, Amazon, or Medium. She has written a historical fiction novel and is looking for an agent. When not writing, Leslie enjoys life with her husband and two naughty Chihuahuas. Together they travel each year from Alabama to Prince Edward Island.*

STANDERD POODELL

BY FAYE UPTON

I'd always known my dad was a scumbag.

Mum never said it in so many words, but she'd never told me who my father was, either. She'd had me at sixteen, and that was a big deal in the Eighties. She fell out with her parents, moved into a nasty bedsit, and abandoned her dreams of going to uni so she could get two jobs and keep her fatherless son in nappies and formula. We spent most of my childhood scraping by. So I never blamed her for not wanting to talk about the toerag who left her pregnant with me in the summer of 1986.

I'll never forget her reaction the first time she found me in my room, laboriously picking out the riff from *Smoke on the Water* on a knockoff Stratocaster. It was the first time I'd ever seen my tough, unflappable, indomitable mum look faint. I was only twelve, I didn't understand, and it never happened again.

But I never forgot.

◆

Standerd Poodell were the biggest band in the world for a while in the late Eighties, but their time at the top didn't last. Fame, fortune, and an astronomical amount of coke saw to that. By the time I was born, nine months after the *Come Into My Parlour* world tour, Standerd Poodell had split up.

I hadn't actually heard of them—not directly. Their hit, *Screamin Mimi,* is one of those tunes you recognize from a hundred ads and trailers without ever knowing the artist, like Fleetwood Mac's *Albatross.* It was a big enough seller, apparently, that all four bandmembers had been in comfortable retirement ever since. For most of my life I could say with reasonable certainty that I'd never laid eyes on any member of Standerd Poodell.

Until that Friday night when, for want of anything else on the TV, I landed on *The Graham Norton Show.*

And when the camera panned over the musical guests—the ageing, drug-addled line-up of Standerd Poodell—and onto lead guitarist Dane Sargent, I realized with a shock that I was looking at my father.

❖

"Holy shit," said Bobby, my drummer, when I showed him the YouTube video at practice the next day. "Holy *shit!*"

"I always thought you looked like Dane Sargent without the mullet," said Leo, our bass player, from his usual position, horizontal on the couch.

"You never said anything."

"No one ever pays attention to the bass player."

"You even play like him," said Leo. "Wearing your Burst low and all."

Bobby snorted. "Yeah, 'cept Matty's Burst is a shitty anniversary copy, not an honest-to-God '59 original with those sweet gold strings."

"Don't trash-talk Jemima," I said, caressing the sunburst finish of my trusty Les Paul Reissue defensively. "And I'd never defile her with gold strings."

"Strings, schmings," said Leo. "That baby of Sargent's is worth five hundred grand. More on the black market."

Bobby paged through Google News. "Whoa. Standerd Poodell's getting back together for a reunion show at the Borderline!"

Leo sat up. "Seriously?"

"It's like a super-secret-VIP-only thing."

"Shit," said Leo. "D'you reckon we could get a support spot?"

"Tony's still booking the Borderline," said Bobby. "And he owes us a favor for what happened in Margate."

"Margate," Leo said with a shudder.

"Wait, you guys," I said. "What makes you think I want anything to do with this Sargent asshole?"

"He's your *dad*," said Leo. "And he might let you jam on his '59."

I flicked a guilty look at Jemima. She was my lady, but a '59 Les Paul was the Holy Grail of electric guitars. "I don't have any proof that he's my sperm donor."

"Yeah?" Bobby took a lip-smacking gulp of his beer and wiggled the bottle at me. "What if you did?"

◆

Tony wouldn't help us. "Line-up's outta my hands."

"C'mon, Tony," Bobby wheedled. "Just get us in the club that night! Moving gear! Sorting M&Ms! Anything!"

"No can do," said Tony. "Get a bleeding ticket."

But there were no tickets to be had. We called everywhere, even the scummy tout sites. Standerd Poodell's reunion gig was strictly invitation-only.

Leo put down the phone. "We're shit outta luck."

"I wouldn't *pay* to see them anyway," I said, clicking the eBay *Bid Now* button.

"Not giving up, are you, Matty?" asked Bobby.

I refreshed my browser. *Congratulations! You won this item!* popped up. "Nope."

The Borderline is a fleapit basement club with sticky carpet, mushy acoustics, and a soundboard held together with expired inspection stickers. We knew it inside out after playing there half a dozen times. All the backstage rooms, all the places on the stage where you'd brain yourself if you jumped too high—and all the ways in and out. There's a front entrance for the customers, a back door for the artists, and a freight lift that makes for dicey load-ins thanks to its habit of breaking down between floors.

It's off Charing Cross Road in Central London, tucked away down a back street. Normally, your average tourist wouldn't even know it's there. But the *super-secret-VIP-only gig* was common knowledge on the Standerd Poodell fan forum (Leo had joined with the handle *whosthedaddy87*). The place would be heaving with Poodell fans. There'd be heavy security. They weren't going to let just anyone in.

But I wasn't going as just anyone.

✦

We started spotting fans as Leo turned our hired Mercedes (complete with fake vanity plates: POO 1) out of Shaftesbury Avenue.

"Jesus Christ," said Bobby, raising his Ray-Bans to gawk. "Talk about ladies of a certain age."

That was putting it mildly. The demographic was north of fifty, which hadn't stopped any of the women tottering down Charing Cross Road in vertiginous white stilettoes from cramming themselves into outfits that had been dubious thirty years ago and hadn't improved for age.

"Don't let 'em catch you," said Leo, honking the horn as a pack of cougars overflowed the pavement. "They'll eat you alive."

I peered into the mirror one last time, tugging my blond wig. "Feel like David Bowie in *Labyrinth*."

"Look like Tina Turner in *Thunderdome*," said Bobby.

"Oi!"

"Keep your lipstick on," said Leo. "We're here."

Five Met police officers were stationed at the Borderline's backstreet rear entrance, holding back the throng. A WPC approached Bobby's passenger side as Leo pulled up, gesturing for him to roll down the window.

"Showtime," said Bobby.

Before the police officer could say a word, I grabbed my guitar case and leapt out of the car.

In hindsight, it wasn't the best idea. I'd gone with the most eye-catching of Sargent's Eighties looks, and the pink pleather pants I'd found on eBay stood out even amongst the sea of dayglo MILFs. The first shriek of "DAAAAANNNNNEEEEEE!" nearly burst my eardrums, and then the herd stampeded toward me.

Thank God for the Met. The police detachment formed a barricade around me, holding back the mob. Bobby jumped out of the car, Ray-Bans back in place above his newly grown goatee, flashing the Sony business card we'd nicked from the TV department of Currys and ordering hysterical women to keep back. I threw enthusiastic devil horns with my left hand and hoped my sunglasses, mullet, and fluorescent makeup would hide that I was clearly thirty years too young to be the real Dane Sargent.

It worked. In the melee, no one looked too closely. The police escorted me through the screaming masses, even opening the steel barriers to let Leo inch the Merc past the security cordon. I clutched my guitar case—decorated to look like Sargent's, with the *READY FOR MY BLOW... DRY!* decal I'd sourced from the Poodell web-shop—as items of female lingerie rained around me.

"Excuse me, Mr. Sargent?" It was the WPC, smiling shyly. "I'm a really big fan. Could I have your autograph?"

"I can't believe we pulled it off," Bobby marveled as we slammed the Borderline's back door.

"We haven't yet," I said, peeling off my wig.

Posing as Sargent to get into the venue was one thing. Inside, the disguise wouldn't work. We'd chosen the dead time between soundcheck and doors-open, when the venue would be mostly empty, but I had to change disguise—fast. A booming clang from outside was Leo loading our gear into the freight lift. Bobby preceded me down the stairs, still in character, as I hopped about, trying to get out of my leopard-print boots.

He hissed at me from the bottom of the stairwell. I froze, half in and half out of my ass-hugging trousers. Then I heard him say, "Yeah, I'm from the label, I've come to check the rider."

The member of staff who'd found him sounded uncertain. "Er, you're supposed to have a security laminate?"

"Yes! Yes, I am! Would you go and get that for me now?"

"Um... okay... come with me..."

Bobby's cover wouldn't hold up for long. I finished shimmying out of the pleather and hurried down the stairs in my underwear.

The gloomy corridor was full of flight cases—empty, by the easy way they rolled. I stood by the lift doors, shifting my weight anxiously as the elevator groaned its way down from street level.

"... not happy with the sound..."

"... pricks are never happy..."

I didn't know the first voice, approaching from around the corner, but I did recognize the second. Tony. If he found me there in my pants, I was finished.

My gaze fell on a Marshall amp case. It would be tight, but I'd fit. (I'd proved it to Bobby once, on a dare.) I stuffed myself inside, pulling the lid down just as Tony and the other speaker came around the corner and the lift clanked to a halt.

"What's this?" asked Tony. "More gear?"

I watched through a gap near the hinges as Tony took my guitar case (containing Jemima) and rucksack (containing my clothes) from the lift.

"Take this to the green room," he told the other guy, handing him my rucksack. "I'll put this on stage."

They left in opposite directions. I gave it a count of ten, then clambered out of the flight case.

I ducked into the mildewy bathroom next to the green room to wipe off my makeup. Then I wrapped one towel around my waist and draped another over my head. Not ideal, but better than pants alone.

As I went to leave, I heard a commotion outside. I drew back.

"... lucky we haven't had you arrested..."

"... get... hands off!"

"... out on your ass... whoever you are..."

They'd rumbled Bobby. But they hadn't recognized him.

I made myself breathe, waited for the fuss to die down, and slipped out of the bathroom.

The green room was empty—of people, at least. I gaped at the spread laid out on the table. When *we* played the Borderline, we were lucky to get a six-pack and some Pringles, but today there was bread, fruit, cold cuts, crudités. The fridge was full of craft beers and wine in real bottles. The bowl of M&Ms actually had all the brown ones taken out.

I spotted my rucksack on the battered leather couch—they hadn't upgraded *that*—and started pulling on clothes: black jeans, black CREW t-shirt, black trainers.

"Who the fuck are you?"

I turned in the act of putting on a baseball cap. "I'm—"

Dane Sargent stood in the doorway.

He had my sandy hair, my blue eyes, my height. Or, I suppose, I had his. Looking at him was like looking into the future, if I planned on wrecking myself with booze and drugs. For him, it must have been like looking into the distant past.

"Well, fuck me," he said, tossing his jacket onto the couch.

It's one thing to see a guy on TV and think he might be your father. It's another to look him in the eye and *know*. I sat down hard on the couch.

"Chip off the old fucking block, aren't you?" Sargent said. He took a Coke from the fridge and took a long gulp. "What do you want? Money?"

I looked up at him. "No."

"'Cause there isn't any. Why'd you think I'm doing this dog-and-pony show?"

"I don't want your money," I said.

"Good." He squinted at me. "How old are you? Thirty?"

"Yeah."

"Another *Parlour* brat. That fucking tour." He pointed to the fridge. "Want a beer?"

"No, thanks," I said. "What do you mean, *another* Parlour *brat*?"

"You think you're my only by-blow from that tour? Kiddo, I was paying for that summer until 2005, and there's *still* more of you bastards crawling out of the woodwork."

"Paying?" I asked stupidly.

"Child support until they were eighteen, and not one fucking day longer."

I sat there, absorbing that, while he chugged his Coke.

"So what do you want?" he asked, crumpling the can and tossing it on the floor.

"I just needed to meet you," I said. "To be certain."

"Well, congratulations, Luke Skywalker. I am your fucking father."

"Do you... remember my mum, at all?"

He gave me a look of flat incredulity. "Are you serious?"

"She was—"

"Don't bother telling me her name. I probably never knew it anyway."

"She was *fifteen*."

"So?"

"You'd have been twenty-eight."

"It was the Eighties. It was probably the best night of her life." Sargent stuck his hand in his pocket. "Here, have this." He thrust something into my hand. "Now if you'll excuse me, I need to take a dump. That fucking vindaloo's messing with my gut something nasty."

I opened my hand as he slouched out. The well-used guitar pick had a pink poodle printed on one side and *GET BLOWN* on the other.

I picked up the crushed Coke can, noticing the flecks of spit around the opening. Saliva and fingerprints. All the evidence I needed to prove that Dane Sargent was, indeed, my father.

I sat there a minute, looking at the pick and can.

"You're not my fucking father," I said, and tossed Sargent's DNA in the bin with the rest of the trash.

On my way out, I ripped the *Access All Areas* lanyard off the jacket Sargent had left on the couch.

❖

Front-of-house was empty but for a single roadie tuning the gold-stringed Les Paul Burst in his lap.

Well, not a roadie exactly. Just Leo. No costume, no disguise, no cover story: just being his invisible, anonymous, unremarkable self.

No one pays attention to the bass player.

"We doing it, then?" he asked.

"Oh, we're doing it," I said.

Leo set the Burst down and picked up a plain black guitar case with only the faintest ghost of glue from a recently removed decal.

As we walked out toward the freight lift, Tony came bustling in. He glanced at us only long enough to spot the AAA laminate hanging around my neck. Then he ignored us.

Leo and I got into the lift in silence. As the door closed, I felt a pang for Jemima. She deserved better.

But so had my mum.

I looked at the nondescript guitar case in Leo's hand.

Five hundred grand would do for starters.

About the Author

Faye Upton is a speculative fiction writer by choice and a regular competitor and semi-regular finalist in NYC Midnight challenges. Faye is also the lead creator of Dragonchoice, *a gargantuan collaborative fanfiction and fanart project spanning twenty-five years, a million-word trilogy of novels, and an online choose-your-own-adventure game.*

She lives in Kent, near London, England, with her silver tabby Raylan. She builds websites for a living. She can't resist a rock musician and once told David Bowie he was rubbish (to his face). Her name can be found on the liner notes of his 2000 live album.

Website: www.dragonchoice.com
Email: feedback@dragonchoice.com
Facebook: snarkmaiden
BlueSky: @strictlydancers.bsky.social

ODESSA

BY R.A. CLARKE

Descending through Trenix's thin upper atmosphere, *The Odyssey's* hull groaned as it sank into the thick band of swirling storm clouds currently swallowing this side of the planet. Normally such inclement weather wouldn't be ideal for gathering rare ingredients, but for the item listed on my collection docket today, this weather was one hundred per cent perfect.

The *sobifacious kliminticus* plant, more commonly known as a sweller swallow, grew here—and only here—and was notoriously hard to find. The troublesome plant was equally difficult to harvest... a unique trait that kept me rich in product orders, since I'd made myself a tidy living doing the dirty work others didn't want to. Sweller swallows were considered a delicacy on nearby planets, thanks to its unique savory flavor and insanely high nutritional value. They had sharp, pearlescent teeth lining the inner side of their blooms, which made great necklace beads, too. Hot sellers all around. I gathered them whenever a product contract carried me to these parts. They kept nicely in cold storage for months, though they never stayed around that long. Though I generally disliked interacting with people, I usually sold out within days.

"And here we are," I said to nobody. There were no crew to squabble with or slow me down. No family or husband to complicate things, which suited me fine. My experience with relationships was that they only led to heartache and bitterness. Growing up in the Reem on my home planet—the grunge district where every crook and scumbag seemed to put roots down—would jade anyone. But if that weren't enough, getting abandoned by my bio birther and adopted out of a tainted foster system to be used by a twisted wraith of a woman clinched it.

She'd beaten the trust and love right out of me.

My ship broke through the broiling cloud ceiling and immediately took a lightning bolt to the starboard side. Spidery electric arcs crackled across my shields for several seconds after the hit but thankfully did little damage. I dove to the planet's surface, punching search commands into the ship's scanners, seeking the nearest gully rich in Trenix clay—the smelly substrate the sweller swallows preferred to grow in.

Despite the payoff, few harvesters wanted to venture to Trenix. Not because the atmosphere wasn't breathable (it was), but because of the horrendous odor. Only a dwindling number of harvesters seemed willing to withstand minor discomfort to earn their rewards these days. Pissed me off no end that my chosen profession was being diluted by pansy-ass up-and-comers, but then again, their lack of work ethic kept me in the money. It also forced me to keep my weapons locker well stocked, since sometimes the lazy buggers switched tactics and jumped on with a pirate crew, then came looking for a quick score. I'd only ever had my cache nicked once. Thankfully, I'd been running light that day. I knew others who'd experienced far worse.

Entire colonies had been pillaged.

The scanner beeped and lit up a section of land on the dashboard's holographic readout. It zeroed in tighter and a target flashed red. "Looks like that's my spot." I prepped for landing and brought the ship down in a nearby meadow.

I could already smell the pungent atmosphere.

When the sun shone, the sky glimmered a vibrant peach and the plentiful trees and wild grasses offered a kaleidoscope of color. Most of the planet was covered in open plains and lush gulleys, with sprawling swaths of forest that, from space, appeared to pockmark the surface. Underground rivers ran all over the place, only surfacing in a handful of locations. However, when it stormed, the clay covering over half the planet's surface turned to sludge and its noxious odor—like a putrid fart sprinkled with skunk spray and dipped in vomit—escaped into the air in full force.

Good thing I'd upgraded my excursion suit with top-notch filtration. This wasn't my twentieth rodeo. *Damn, has it really been twenty years? I've been doing this for half my life.*

I'd already walked down the exit ramp before realizing I'd forgotten the ship's ignition fob, with the keys to my cargo lockers attached. Leaving those behind was like inviting someone to steal my shit. Though the ramp was rising behind me, I activated the magnet recoil function on my tool belt. I heard the whir before I saw the keys zip through the narrowing gap to *kachink* into their rightful place on my belt. I grinned as the ramp sealed shut.

"Alright, let's do this." I tightened the clasp, keeping my silver-streaked sienna hair out of my face, secured my helmet, and headed out of the meadow toward the stand of scattered trees ahead. A forest rested beyond that, growing out of a rich clay deposit. My quarry would be in this area without a doubt. The rain made them much easier to spot, as it gave their usually matte camouflage skin an oily sheen that created rainbow swirls. Without that, the only way to know they were there, lying in wait, was to see their antenna—if it rose up—a stem about the width of a spaghetti noodle with a teeny ball on top. Its eye. Spotting that meant you were in attack range.

Near constant rolls of thunder filled the atmosphere, laying waste to silence.

I still felt the ache in my knees from my last harvest, where I'd had to snowshoe through icy drifts to collect the summit blooms native to planet Valreeth's frozen wasteland. My joints weren't nearly as happy with my daredevil job as my mind these days. At forty, I was considered old for a harvester. And while I knew someday

I'd grudgingly have to seek out alternative sources of income, I remained resolute... That wouldn't be happening anytime soon.

With my scanner in one hand, calibrated to seek rainbow patterns, and my combustor gun in the other, I threaded between the trees. My mind wandered, considering employment options once my harvesting days were over. No way could I do any kind of desk job—too much sitting around. Farming could be good. I didn't mind animals. They were easy to understand, didn't lie. Or maybe I could work with children, young girls that needed help. I could ensure others didn't suffer my fate, turned into slaves, innocence lost. Give them some hope, a fighting chance.

I shook the thoughts away. *Now's not the time. Focus.*

As I made my way deeper into the forest, I patiently waited for a sign that told me a target was nearby... then less patiently when none came. "Where are all of you?"

As if on cue, my scanner beeped.

"Finally..." I turned to my right, zeroing in on the red kidney-bean shaped patch that glowed on my screen. It wasn't far away.

Beep.

Another red glow appeared a few feet beyond the first. *Two for one. Nice.*

The moody skies continued rumbling as searing lightning bolts snaked across the clouds. The faintest *whooshing* noise reached my ears, capturing my attention, but when it blended in with the gusting wind, I wrote it off as such.

After one last sweep of the area with the scanner—a necessary precaution, as sweller swallows were known to crowd in and creep closer when prey was near—I secured the device on my belt and whipped out a shock baton. "Time to dance."

Their antennas weren't raised now. But the sneaky devils would've seen me coming for a while already. Luckily, they weren't smart enough to know I'd seen them, too.

I crept closer, waiting for my moment.

My grip tightened on the baton.

"Come on out," I cooed. "I won't—"

The first plant swelled, rising from the muddy ground on a six-foot-tall purple stem. Its two rounded petals splayed wide like wings, their deep red surfaces marred with shiny spades. A web of thick green veins pulsed and merged into a maw-like throat.

"—bite!" I thrust the shock baton into the mud and used it to catapult my legs into the air as the business end sent a wave of electricity into the wet soil. The shock rippled out, colliding with the base of the unruly plant. It shuddered and snapped haphazardly, as if confused about where I was. It presented the tender section of stem just below its bloom, and I fired off a round as my feet hit the ground, severing it.

The second sweller rose as the head of the first tipped and toppled into the muck. It slithered its slug-like base toward me.

A strange mewling sound wafted to my ears, then vanished in the wind. It had come from somewhere behind me. I looked back, seeing nothing.

The sweller snapped at me, but I jolted back just in time. "Dammit," I growled, chiding myself for the near miss. "Pay attention."

The scanner on my belt beeped, but I had no time to check it as the bloodthirsty plant darted forward for another try. Jumping to the side, I swung my baton behind me, rewarded by a tug. The sweller's head squeezed down on the shaft, grinding its deadly petals together.

I sent a shock through it and it recoiled, flailing its stem and shaking leaves back. With its neck fatally exposed, I took the shot.

A shadow rose over me. *Shit.*

I turned just in time to thrust my gun into the surging mouth of a third plant. The shot hammered its core and blew out the other side, but hadn't severed its stem. It lurched backward as if on a spring and swung back around. I jumped to the side, landing in a roll as its head slammed into the mud where I had stood a second before. Contorting my arm, I fired, beheading it.

Climbing to my feet, I ripped my scanner off my belt, holding it out. "Any more takers?" There was no sign of others close by, but that didn't mean I was safe. There'd be more in the vicinity and they'd be heading this way. In the meantime, I surveyed my kills and smiled.

"Not bad for a day's work. Should fetch a fair credit." I pulled a foot-long cylindrical tube off my belt and activated my auto-cart—a floating wheelbarrow made of force fields—and tossed the three heads into it.

That mewling sound reached my ears again, but it had changed. It was louder this time, shriller, like a warbling cry.

No, not *like* a cry. It *was* a cry.

That sounded like a baby.

"What the—?" I glanced toward the sound, but it was hard to tell where it originated. The wind kept stealing it away, and it echoed off the trees. Thunder rolled overhead, muffled by the broiling clouds unleashing fresh sheets of rain.

And there it was again, now crisp between gusts. Screams of rage or fear.

Or pain.

The cry intensified and a slew of worst-case scenarios filled my mind, gritty images flashing like exploding bombs. What was a friggin' baby doing out here? I knew if I could hear the child, so could the swellers. A memory flashed through my mind, acrid and festered. Being left by the wraith in a greasy tavern slithering with scuzzy pervs, ordered not to come home without cash in my pocket. I grimaced, remembering what I'd endured to earn my keep...

I gripped my auto-cart and strode back toward the grassy meadow I'd landed in, confident that's where it was coming from. A gnawing sense of dread seeped in from the darkest parts of me, then simmered into a boil of anger. My fists clenched, knuckles white. *Abandoned. Vulnerable. Used.* Unable to come up with any logistical or wholesome reason why a baby would be brought to Trenix, I broke into a run, simultaneously listening for any beeps from my scanner. The cart sailed weightlessly behind me.

I knew I was breaking my own rules. I'd sworn long ago to not get involved in other people's drama, that I would leave the world to its filth and just focus on my own shit. But I couldn't help myself. I'd never been a very maternal woman, but something pulled at me like a magnet, screaming injustice, danger. I couldn't live with myself if I didn't investigate.

Beep. Beep.

I checked my scanner. The plants were far enough away that I could give them a wide berth. On a normal day, I'd never pass up the chance to harvest, but given this unexpected and downright bizarre situation, normalcy had flown out the window.

I veered left, the sound now leading me away from the meadow I'd parked my ship in. Hot sweat beaded on my brow as I ran, weaving from side to side to avoid triggering more flora. They seemed less intent on me, anyway. Likely salivating in response to those cries, their still-flattened forms slithered in the same direction I was moving. Not good.

I glowered as the baby wailed again—so close now. "I better find some parents, and they better have a damn good reason for bringing their kid here."

Beep.

A huge sweller rose right in front of me. I gasped, and without thinking, swung the auto-cart around. The netted force fields hammered into its thick stem, rocking it backward. I shot twice for good measure, destroying its neck. The head fell in a heap and I swiftly scooped it up, dropping it into the cart. I pressed forward, pushing my way through a thicket of willowy bushes, then emerged into another clearing.

I came to an abrupt stop, bewildered.

Knee-high wild grasses whipped in the wind and lightning flashed overhead. A sizable rectangular boulder surrounded by several smaller bulbous ones sat near the heart of the meadow. The top of the biggest was about four feet tall and somewhat flat. Good thing, because an infant was lying on top of it. The little thing was nestled in a blanket, its cherubic face pale and soaked by rain. I wasn't an expert on children, but if I had to guess, it was only months old.

I looked in all directions, seeing no one.

Nothing about this felt right.

Abandoned. Used.

Rage flared within, protective and raw. It warred with my good sense, the voice in my head telling me to turn away—to remember my rules and abide by them. But I couldn't leave the child there to die. The poor thing was a sitting duck, a free meal for the sweller swallows.

I could at least get it somewhere safe. Clutching my gun, I pulled my cart into the meadow, eyes darting warily in search of movement, people, antennas, anything.

My scanner remained silent as I reached the rock. The baby's face was red from screaming, lips purple from the cold. Its tiny arms and legs jerked angrily within the sopping blanket. A pale pink jumper marked with a strange symbol—like three stars offset from each other—poked out from between the folds.

"Shhh..." I released the auto-cart, leaving it hovering behind me, and brushed one of my fingers down her cheek. "You're okay now. You're not alone anymore."

The infant's eyes found me. Her cry faltered a moment while staring up at my unfamiliar face, then carried on. I glanced around and checked my scanner. The swellers would come soon, slowed only slightly by the bushes I'd just fought through. I wanted to shout out to see if, by some miracle, a blundering set of parents was close by, but an alarm went off in my head at the thought. The baby had been set too perfectly, like a sacrifice placed upon an altar.

Something stunk about this situation and it wasn't the soil.

You're smarter than this. Walk away.

Instead of listening to my own advice, however, I curled both hands beneath the baby and lifted her off the rock, cradling her against my chest. Though the blanket was wet, I bunched it up over the top of her in a way to help shield her from the rain. She was so light and tiny, and I found it was an odd experience to hold such a tiny being. A hint of fear swept through me, and discomfort at the notion I might somehow injure her. I let the child grip one of my fingers and cooed softly as my eyes darted around the meadow. Her cry soon lessened, then fizzled into stuttering sniffles.

"There now…" While looking at her cherubic face, I decided to take the risk and call out. It was a long shot, but the parents could have fallen prey to a sweller attack. They could be somewhere out of view needing help. And if they were present, they simply had to be found. Goodness knew, I wasn't equipped to care for a baby for more than a few moments. My ship wasn't prepped, nor did I have nearly enough knowledge to feel remotely competent.

I opened my mouth to shout, but then paused, remembering the odd whooshing sound I'd heard before. It was a sound that didn't glaringly stand out, and yet didn't fit in either. It was an anomaly—an unexplained one. Perhaps that hadn't been wind after all. Given the fact there was a damn baby here in the middle of a sweller-filled meadow, it could have been another ship.

It might just be other harvesters. But again, why bring a baby? And worse, why leave a baby behind? Such a thing was unheard of. Nothing about this made any sense. *Unless…*

"If you hand over the cart and unlock your ship, you and the wee babe can go free." The deep, raspy voice rang out from the tree line and my eyes snapped toward it.

Across the clearing, a wiry-framed man in a ragged military-style hat, grimy britches, and an armless leather jacket that exposed the pistols holstered across his broad chest stepped out from where he'd been hiding amongst the foliage. He removed his simplistic filtration mask and shone me a sly smile, revealing a full grille of silver-capped teeth.

Three more equally disheveled men in similar attire appeared behind their leader, each one squinting one beady eye as they pointed their guns at me.

Pirates...

My gun flew up, trained on the boss.

"What kind of heartless creatures are you to use a defenseless baby as bait?" Teeth gritted, my eyes bore into them. "Whose baby is this? Yours?"

He held his hands up. "Goodness no. That's just some kid we inherited during a colony raid. Was locked in a cage. You wanna talk heartless? That's about as cold as it gets. We figured there'd be some use for it down the line, and voila—turns out there was."

My mind spun. *A cage... Used.*

"How did you follow me here? My ship didn't detect you on scanners."

"Oh, we have our ways..." The leader continued strolling forward, undeterred by my aimed weapon. "We've been watching you for a while now. You've been making waves in the harvesting world. Bringing in big credit hauls." He snickered. "I'd say it's high time we took our share of the spoils. An easy trade, little lady."

Chauvinistic asshole.

"My spoils are just that—*my* spoils. I earned them, so you can fuck off."

He laughed, glancing at his buddies. "Is that any way to talk to the men who have three guns trained on you?" He *tsk tsk*'d, then raised his own weapon, letting out a cackle. "Correction. Make that four guns. Now unlock your ship."

A faint rustling noise wafted to my ears. Flicking my gaze around the clearing, I keyed in on several antennas watching quietly, inconspicuous amidst the grass. The swellers were here.

Do the pirates know about the plants here?

Thinking on my feet, I shifted the baby, using the action as a shield while my other hand turned off the scanner I knew would start beeping very soon. Though that left me vulnerable, at least I wouldn't show the only cards I was likely to hold in this scenario. In my distracted state, they'd gotten the drop on me dead to rights, a fact I despised but couldn't help now. I held my ground, thrusting my chin high. "No. Just turn around and leave now, and nobody gets hurt."

The baby gripped my finger tighter, as if she also sensed the danger we faced.

The leader fired a shot and the laser-like pulse seared into my arm just inches above the baby's tender scalp. I jerked back, failing to swallow a sharp, pain-filled shout. Glancing down quickly, I confirmed two things. First, it truly had *not* hit the baby, and second, it was just a flesh wound. *Fucker.* That had come too close to hitting the defenseless bundle in my tenuous care.

"Next one, the baby gets it."

Though I'd consider myself the furthest thing from good mother material, whatever shriveled remnants of a heart I had left were reserved solely for those who were vulnerable. Like I'd been once. Only, back then, there was nobody who cared enough to take a risk and help me escape the nasty situations I grew up dealing with. Unlike the folks who failed me, I wasn't about to fail this kid. I wouldn't play with this child's life, no matter where she might've come from.

"Okay, okay…" I holstered my gun, panting from the burn in my arm.

He shook his head. "No, drop it."

Stifling a growl, I let my gun fall to the ground and raised my free hand to shoulder height, gently patting the baby with the other. Every now and then she let out little gurgling sounds, blowing spit bubbles with her mouth. Not a care in the world. *Must be nice.* I spared one quick glance down only to see her bright gray eyes staring back at me. At that moment, something deep and ingrained within my hardened, world-weary core crumbled.

"Kick it away."

I nodded, booting my combustor a few feet out of reach. That would be a problem. Glancing around, I noticed several more antennas perking up amidst the grass. Some had slunk closer, inching their way slowly forward. Stalking. They would be more problems.

"Thank ye kindly." The man gave a gallant nod. "Now unlock your ship."

I shook my head, keeping my free hand well raised. "I can't remotely unlock anything." The leader narrowed his eyes, scrunching up one side of his face. But I continued, "Seriously. She's an old-school ship. The lockers in the cargo hold all still have keys." I slowly lowered my hand, and the pirates stiffened with alert, thrusting their guns forward.

"Easy now. Take a breath." Leveling my gaze on the leader, I added, "Just let me give you the keys, and then you can go raid it, okay? Take all the goods I have stocked up in there. It's yours. I'll just take the kid like you said, and we both win."

He seemed suspicious, lips pursing as he seemed to consider the deal. "Maybe we should take your ship, too. Eh, girlie? Might fetch a nice purse from a collector or another harvester. We should just kill you now and be done with it. No strings attached. Whaddya say, boys?"

The man's wolf pack cackled, nodding along like a bunch of mindless followers.

Girlie? This asshole was really starting to try my patience, and I didn't possess too much of that to begin with. I raised both my eyebrows in challenge. "We both know you won't do that."

The leader slanted a look my way. "Oh, really... and why's that?"

"'Cause I'm worth more to you alive than dead. I bring in the biggest hauls around. The most dangerous flora and fauna. You said so yourself—I've been making waves. You leave me here to die and you'll be short-changing yourself." His head tilted. I had his interest. "We could make an ongoing deal instead. Split profits or something. Besides, that ship's not worth much—it's outdated and needs constant fixing—a glorified tin can. If I could afford to upgrade to a new model, I would have already." I forced a wistful look to hide my lie. "That's a someday plan."

"Hmm." The leader picked at his teeth, hemming and hawing before re-securing his face mask. He glanced at each of his lackeys, two of which shrugged, tossing the ball back to him.

The tallest of the three spoke up. "Makes sense to me, Dagen."

Dagen. It was good to put a name to the face.

"Yeah, and if she tries to ghost us, we kill her," the chubby one chimed in.

The baby yawned, releasing the most adorable sound. The sheer cuteness of it was distracting, but I shook my head, remaining focused. Both of our lives depended on the outcome of this moment. "I won't ghost you. Look, let me toss you the keys." The baby then grumbled, and I had the silliest thought that maybe she didn't agree with what I was doing. I kind of felt like giving her the stink-eye and telling her, *this is all because of you, so you better be thankful.*

I just hoped the hastily hatched plan I was unfurling wasn't a foolhardy one.

"Well, go on then. Toss 'em." Dagen motioned his gun for me to get my keys.

I fumbled to detach my ignition fob and held it up. A gust of wind blew, jangling the metallic slivers attached to it. "Alright? Here are my damn keys." Under the guise of an eye roll, I glanced to the left, sourcing the closest and thickest clump of antennas.

Dagen gave me a *gimme* hand gesture. A sly smile twitched on his mouth. So smug and proud of himself. Over my dead body would he ever get *The Odyssey.*

Here goes nothing. I cocked my arm back and hurled the key fob into the grass about fifteen feet away from the pirate assholes.

Hoping for a distraction, I jerked to the side, making for the boulder's protection, but a shot zinged past my torso, leaving a charred starburst on the rock. I froze again, thrusting my hand back in the air.

"You stupid cow! Don't you move," Dagen shouted, glaring at me. He waved a crisp arm to his men, then pointed to the area my keys had fallen. "Go find them." The barrel of his gun never wavered from its aim.

"Can't blame a girl for trying," I called.

The three lackeys went trudging toward the keys, grumbling and glowering back at me. The baby squirmed. I squeezed her tighter, my arm cramping from being in the same position for too long. "Shh now... everything's fine," I murmured, ignoring the discomfort. Though locked in a staring match with Dagen, I watched his men spreading out to search from the corner of my eye. The antennas in the grass had disappeared from view.

"Come on, come on," I breathed, so quiet I doubted even the baby heard it.

A sweller swallow sprang up just two feet from the largest of the pirate minions. He shouted in horror and pelted it with shots. None of them found the sweet spot, and the flower's maw snapped down on his arm. He screamed, the teeth ripping into his flesh. The other men turned and let rounds fly, then spun circles as four more swellers rose up around them.

Hell yes.

"Fall back!" Dagen shouted, his gun swinging between me and his crew in halted motions, clearly torn about what to do. But when a sweller chomped down on the short chubby guy's shoulder and lifted him up off his feet—blood spurting—he made his choice. Dagen turned, aiming his weapon at the flowers.

I darted for my gun on the ground, then slid behind the boulder. After carefully setting the child down on the grass next to the rock where she'd gain some semblance of protection, my eyes flicked in every direction. There were zero antennas visible around me now. A bad sign.

They were close.

I looked down. "Alright, baby, get ready for a fight. We're getting outta this place."

Reactivating my scanner, I held it up. All I had to do was clear a path out of the meadow, then get my ass back to the ship. Correction, *our* asses.

Screams splintered the air. I spared a glance toward the pirates. Dagen had charged toward the flowers, but smartly hung back, sending rapid-fire shots. He tagged one with a lucky shot, severing its head, but didn't change his haphazard firing pattern. One of his guys was already dead. The other was only half visible—his bloody upper torso hanging listlessly out of a massive sweller's mouth. Its robust stem stretched while the flower gnawed his body, swallowing him whole like an anaconda. More swellers popped up, blocking the pirates' retreat.

Beep, beep.

The wind whipped the grass in a frenzy, but I caught a flash of an oily rainbow to my right just as the scanner marked it. Another one glowed on my left. More were incoming from the tree line, but they veered away, drawn to the hearty feast of pirates currently staining the grass red. Dropping my scanner, I snatched my baton and lunged forward, taking the fight to the swellers. The first one sprang as I dove into a slide across the slick grass, thrusting my baton into its base and letting the electricity fly. It jerked and shuddered as I fired a round straight up into its throat.

Amidst the screaming and gunshots across the meadow, I heard the second one spring behind me on the other side. My throat constricted. It had moved faster than expected. *The baby.*

Scrambling to my feet, I rushed back, but the flower head was already surging down toward the ground, aiming for the child.

"No!" I cried out, hitting the steady stun function and throwing my baton at the sweller. It missed by a fraction, its metallic tip *tinging* off the rock instead.

The baby let out a piercing wail as the flower's teeth closed in on her tiny, helpless form, and something seized inside my chest. I lunged forward, knowing full well I'd never make it in time. But I had to try—to move. I couldn't just sit idly by and watch it steal her newborn life.

But then something unexpected happened. Strangely, the flower's surging head slowed. I didn't hesitate. A guttural scream ripped from my lips as I threw my body into the stem to knock it off course, and it worked. The sweller swung to the side with me hanging on, then rebounded back like a whip to dislodge me.

I tumbled through the grass, ending up several feet away. Too far. I'd be too late. Clambering back to my feet, I glimpsed Dagen swarmed by flora, but I ignored it—my focus set on saving the baby. But as I charged again, the vision I encountered halted my footsteps.

My sweaty skin stretched as my expression twisted in confusion. *What the—?*

The sweller had ceased its attack.

Its splayed sinewy petals fluttered slowly as they hovered above the child, twisting from one side to the other, kind of like a puppy might when it was curious. Never in all my years of harvesting had I ever seen one of these deadly, merciless plants ever resist a meal.

Fresh screams sliced through the rain.

I knew Dagen was in trouble, but I didn't look. He wasn't my concern. He was a user, selfish and callous, just like all the scum that paid for my painfully young self to go into their rooms back at the bar. Whatever was happening over there, the guy had it coming to him.

Inching forward, I approached the boulder cautiously from the side. What could've possibly made the sweller stop? As I neared, fearing what I might see, I finally got a clearer look at the child, whose urgent cry had lessened a degree. Had some other local critter I couldn't see entered the equation, or was she fortuitously lying in something repellant to swellers?

The moment the infant's face came into clear view, my hand instinctively flew to cover my mouth, but ended up slapping awkwardly against my face shield instead.

The baby was smiling up at the plant, her head tilting side to side right along with it. But what had me sucking in a sharp breath was the color of her eyes. The child's irises weren't gray anymore, but instead, iridescent flecks of green shone within their depths—like two shimmering, almost neon, emeralds. Was it possible the plant was doing that to her?

Or was *she* doing that to the plant?

The sweller suddenly twisted toward me, my presence breaking into its placid trance-like state. It snapped at me and I jumped back just in time. But before I could even raise my gun to fire, hoping to stun it enough to allow for evasive maneuvers, the baby's piercing cry erupted into a new level of shrill. The scream made me wince, and immediately the sweller froze.

Its blossom's head swiveled back to the baby, submissive.

"Holy shit…" I scrambled back to my feet.

"Help! Please!" Dagen wailed from afar.

A quick glance revealed one of his arms hung uselessly at his side. Ruby droplets fell from it, scattered onto the nearby grasses by the wind. He spun in circles, firing shots with his single functioning hand, ducking and diving away from vicious bites. One toothy bloom sunk its teeth deep into his leg and he screamed, losing his footing in a frantic bid to free himself.

Cringing, I knew it would be over quickly.

I looked down at the baby as I tried to ignore the carnage. Tried to ignore the sounds. But something within her bizarre glowing eyes spurred an unwelcome measure of empathy to claw its way to the surface. I growled aloud as pity followed, too strong to ignore, the irking sensation far too much like weakness for my tastes. Such a wretch didn't deserve to be helped. He deserved to die. And yet, in the next second, I bellowed out, "Shoot the stems at the base of the blooms!" *There. That's all he gets.* I didn't wait to see if he heard me or if he'd be able to action the tip.

Cautiously, I dipped down to scoop up the infant, tensing when the flower head jerked toward me. However, the baby's cry surged again, and the sweller stilled, its stalk vibrating as though such an act of restraint required a Herculean effort to maintain.

I stepped away with the child, reclaiming and re-holstering my shock baton, then tossed the sweller's head I'd severed into my waiting auto-cart. "Time to go." I tucked my scanner into the hand holding the baby, able to support her easily enough within the crook of my arm, and then pulled my cart out of the clearing, leaving Dagen to his fate.

My scanner beeped several more times as we rushed back to the ship, but thankfully, I was able to steer clear of any other toothy assailants. In the back of my mind, I wondered, with an equal mix of awe and trepidation, if the little one could command more of the sweller swallows—or maybe all of them—but I sure wasn't about to try to test the theory.

I broke out of the trees and into the meadow I had landed in, smiling with acute relief at the sight of my old ship still sitting there, ready to fly. There was no visible sign the pirates had tampered with it, but I'd know for sure once I ran a quick diagnostic sweep from the cockpit.

I reached for my key fob, but found it wasn't there. "Crap..." In the rush to vacate, I'd forgotten to retrieve it. Hitting the magnet recoil on my belt, I waited, hoping it functioned from such a distance. I'd never tested it from so far before, and I silently willed for it to work.

Come on, come on.

The baby had stopped crying by then and looked up at me, gurgling and blowing an array of spit bubbles. Inexplicably, her irises had returned to their original gray shade. I found myself staring and questioning whether I'd only imagined her eyes glowing.

Though I was still very confused and detoxing from the rush of adrenaline, I managed a smile. "Thank you for helping me out back there, you know, with the sweller—er, that *flower monster*. You sure are a mysterious little one. But I bet you know that already, don't you?" I shook my head, letting out a low chuckle. The baby squealed, waving her hands around, and it was then I noticed a tremble in her little limbs. I needed to get her warm.

A whirring noise reached my ears.

Within seconds, the fob zoomed through the trees, sending tattered leaves flying before it slammed back into my tool belt. "Yes! Oh, thank goodness." With a tired grin, I pulled the fob off my belt and unlocked the ship, lowering the loading ramp. I promptly guided the auto-cart inside and secured it in cold storage.

Next, I carried the drenched infant into my living quarters and laid her on the bed.

Not having the faintest clue what to do with a newborn, I dried her off the best I could and then wrapped her up in a t-shirt. It was a garish, makeshift swaddle job, but at least it would be dry and warm. "Well, I guess I'll have to give you a name now, too. I mean, I could just call you *Baby*, but that doesn't feel right. A—" I struggled for the right word, knowing she looked very human, but might not be at all "—*being* as unique as you deserves a good name."

I glanced up at the wall my bed rested against, thinking of options. The smooth metal surface was slathered with old relic photos I'd saved as a child, ones portraying happy people in loving families I once dreamed of having—idyllic images that got me through years of hell until the last vestiges of hope died. I kept them up to serve as a reminder for me to stay strong and rely on nobody but myself. And yet, as I looked at them now, I found myself wishing their smiles were mine. I gave my head a shake.

"Ugh, what is going on with me? I'm seeing babies with green eyes and helping a *pirate*... I think I need a stiff drink and some sleep."

The baby half squealed, half giggled.

My lips twitched. "You think I'm funny, do you?" As I ran a hand through my disheveled hair, my gaze landed on the framed pilot's certificate hanging over my desk beside a tarnished steel placard bearing the ship's name and manufacturer information. *The Odyssey...*

I looked back down. "How about Odessa? That has a nice ring to it. Do you like that?"

The baby cooed, grabbing at her feet within the fabric in an undeniably cute way.

"A toe grab—I'll take that as a yes." I lifted her up and carried her into the cockpit, where I settled her into an open cargo box lined with blankets. "It ain't pretty, but it will do for now. Alright, Odessa. Let's get the hell–er, *heck* out of here, find you something to eat, and then sell us some swellers. Might as well make this mess of a trip worthwhile, right?" As I fired up the engine, an alien sense of comfort struck. For the first time in many years, I was not alone.

And that actually felt... good.

Odessa blew more raspberries, and I couldn't help but grin, tickling her little belly. "Then we'll get you back home safe and sound, okay? Wherever that is. We'll figure it out together. I promise." But then I thought of what the pirates had said—that they'd found the baby locked in a cage on some colony. *A damn cage.* My jaw clenched, and I swallowed hard, conflicted.

Cutting through the storm clouds, I hit some buttons on the flight board and took the ship up into the atmosphere, angling for the winking stars beyond. As the jostling eased and a blanket of inky blackness enveloped *The Odyssey*, I couldn't stop thinking about what this child's future might hold. What kind of trouble it might bring. What if her makers, if that's what I should call them, came looking? I certainly couldn't let her to go back into a cage, nor could I stomach leaving her fate to chance by dumping her into any kind of foster care system.

I looked at Odessa's chubby cheeks, then into those mysterious gray eyes, and that foreign sensation of comfort intensified. It was unnerving, yet tranquil, oddly warm.

I squeezed one of her feet. "Or... maybe you're already home."

About the Author

R.A. Clarke is a former police officer turned stay-at-home mom from Portage la Prairie, MB. She shares life with a sport-aholic husband, two adorable boys, and an ever-expanding collection of novels-in-progress. Besides coffee, acting, and lake time, R.A. enjoys plotting multi-genre fiction, and creating children's books as Rachael Clarke.

She has won international short story competitions such as The Writer's Workout Writer's Games, Writers Weekly 24-Hour Short Story Contest, and Red Penguin Books' humor contest. In 2021, she was named a Hindi's Libraries Females of Fiction finalist and a Futurescapes Award finalist, as well as a Dark Sire Award finalist in 2022. Her novella Becoming Grace *won the Write Fighters 3-Day Novella Challenge in 2023. R.A.'s work can be purchased anywhere books are sold.*

To learn more, visit www.rachaelclarkewrites.com or follow her socials at linktr.ee/raclarkewrites.

ACKNOWLEDGEMENTS

Thanks to all the writers from my two online groups who've trusted us with their story babies in *Thief,* the first Salty Dog Press anthology. We hope there'll be more.

Thanks, as ever, to Andy for being my partner in life and in (stories of) crime. He had a blast reading these wonderful tales and has been a vital support in our exciting new publishing venture. It's our aim to lift and give something back to writers, a group doing it tough in these 'post' times—post-literature, post-television, post-cinema. Post-everything-except-the-phone.

Keep at it, folks. There may be fewer readers around, but stories will always be magic.

ABOUT THE EDITOR

Paulene Turner is the owner of Salty Dog Press and is the author of a six-book YA series, The Time Travel Chronicles. A former journalist, she also writes short stories and novellas—some of which have appeared in anthologies and magazines in the UK, US and Australia. As well as writing short plays, she directs them for Short and Sweet, Sydney.

She lives in Sydney, Australia with her husband, twin daughters and twin pugs.

To read more of her stories, find links to purchase her books or subscribe to her mailing list, and for news on new projects:

Visit Paulene's website

www.pauleneturnerwrites.com

Like and follow Paulene on

Facebook: facebook.com/pauleneturnertimetraveller

Instagram: instagram.com/pauleneturnertimetraveller

TikTok: tiktok.com/@pauleneturnertimetravels

X: x.com/PauleneTurner

ALSO BY PAULENE TURNER

The Time Travel Chronicles

Secrets of the Nile
Revenge of the Black Knight
Shoot-out at Death Canyon
Black Tides
Samurai Steal
Point of Origin

Collection

Heartbeats—short stories with a dash of love